Olivia

Brides of Montana

Book Six

Cheryl Wright

Olivia

Brides of Montana – Book Six

Copyright ©2022

by Cheryl Wright

Small Town Romance Publications

Dedication

To Margaret Tanner, my very dear friend and fellow author, for her enduring encouragement and friendship.

To Alan, my husband of over forty-nine years, who has been a relentless supporter of my writing and dreams for many years.

To You, my wonderful readers, who encourage me to continue writing these stories. It is such a joy knowing so many of you enjoy reading my stories as much as I love writing them for you.

Table of Contents

Chapter One

Grand Falls, Montana – 1880's

The last thing Joseph Davis expected when he stepped outside his store was to collide with a total stranger.

"I apologize," he said as he steadied her, but the woman stared at him blankly before continuing along the boardwalk.

Something was amiss, but Joseph did not know what it was. He hurried after her and spoke gently as he walked beside her. "Miss," he said, turning to face her. "You seem to be poorly. How can I help?" She appeared out of sorts, and didn't seem to know what was going on around her. It was as though she was in another world.

It wasn't something Joseph would normally do, but he grabbed her by both arms and stared into her face. Her expression didn't change, she didn't blink, and didn't react in any way. Strangely, she continued to walk. Or at least she tried. It bothered Joseph, and he moved aside.

By now, they had almost reached the Apothecary. Perhaps he could get Jesse to come and check on her. Joseph knew it wasn't his business, but she was clearly in some kind of difficulty, and he couldn't, in good faith, leave the woman to her own devices.

He ran ahead and ducked his head around the door. "Jesse," he said urgently. "I need your help. There's a woman outside who appears to be in a trance."

Before he could say more, Jesse rushed out the door. "Miss?" he said as he studied her, but had no response. Jesse shook his head at Joseph. "We need to get her inside and sit her down. She appears to be in shock."

It took the strength of both men to direct her inside and sit her down. Joseph then ran for the sheriff's office. As much as he felt bad for the woman, this was the most excitement their little town had experienced for a very long time.

Sheriff Earl Saxon pushed his hat back off his head. "She doesn't look familiar at all. If the lady was a criminal, I'd have a wanted poster."

"Oh, come on, Sheriff. Does she look like a criminal to you?" Joseph couldn't believe what he was hearing. This woman was well dressed, although there were small tears here and there, and her hair was rather disheveled. She clutched tightly to her reticule, and the sheriff's eyes had drifted toward it several times now.

The sheriff chuckled. "What is a criminal supposed to look like?" He had a point, but Joseph said nothing. "If we can get her to my office, I'll make enquiries."

Jesse intervened. "No disrespect to you, Sheriff, but I don't think that's going to work. What she needs is rest. Perhaps we can get Doc Spencer to take her to the surgery. He can give her far better care than I can here."

Without warning, the woman suddenly stood, still clutching her reticule. "Where…where am I?" She shook her head, glanced at each man standing nearby, then her expression changed to terror. Suddenly, she ran. She fumbled opening the door, and the sheriff grabbed her before she could leave.

"You're a bit rough, don't you think, Sheriff? The lady has done nothing wrong." Joseph was beginning to regret his part in bringing the sheriff to her aid. So far, he hadn't helped, only accused.

Sheriff Saxon glared at him. "We don't know if that's true," he almost growled, still holding onto her.

"What is your name?" Joseph asked gently, not wanting to frighten her further.

She closed her eyes momentarily, then answered. "Olivia S…Foster. I escaped from my kidnappers." Tears rolled down her face then, and without warning, she collapsed in a heap.

Joseph couldn't believe what he was hearing. *Kidnappers? Exactly who was this woman? And what was she doing here in Grand Falls?* There were no kidnappers here. At least he didn't think there were.

Grand Falls was a quiet town. The sheriff did little because of that fact. He mostly sat in his office looking at wanted posters, or wandering around town socializing with the townfolk. He wasn't a young man, but he wasn't old either. It was a job Joseph wouldn't like – he'd far prefer to be busy.

His job as a bootmaker meant he had a tranquil life, as he wasn't overburdened with orders. On the other hand, he had enough work to keep him happy. He couldn't ask for anything more.

As he pounded the leather of the boots he was making, Joseph felt himself calming down. He hadn't realized how enraged he'd become hearing her words. He wondered if the sheriff had found out who she was and what had happened to her.

Joseph may never know.

The door to his store opened, and he hurried from his workroom out to the store. It surprised him to see the young woman standing there. She looked far more alert now that she had earlier.

She glanced up as he approached her. "Thank you," she blurted out. "The sheriff said you were the one who noticed me and got help." Her hands fidgeted, as though she couldn't stop herself.

"I did what anyone would do." She appeared quite agitated as she continued to twist her hands this way and that. "Are you all right?" Joseph suddenly asked. Tears welled in her eyes, and without warning, she turned and ran out of the store.

There was no doubt in his mind there was more to this woman than it appeared. The biggest question Joseph had was how did she get to town? She said she'd been kidnapped. If that was the case, how did she escape?

He shook himself. The last thing Joseph wanted was to be caught up in something untoward. *Did the sheriff still have suspicions she might be entangled in criminal activity?* She seemed such a normal woman – apart from the fact she claimed to have been kidnapped.

Joseph returned to his workroom but couldn't concentrate. Her visit had induced more questions than answers. He pulled off his leather apron and headed out of the store. He would go for a walk to clear his head. Perhaps then he might be able to concentrate on more than the events of a short time ago.

He stepped outside as he had done earlier, only this time, he was alone. A stranger didn't collide with him, and he was free to wander as he pleased. Considering that, Joseph headed toward the park. It would be nice to sit in the gazebo and just take in the quiet and the fresh air. It wasn't often he managed to do so. Especially on work days.

He'd not long sat down, and the same woman from this morning appeared. "Hello again," she said.

"Hello," he said gruffly. Her presence wasn't exactly welcomed. He'd felt quite agitated since their earlier encounter. Why that was, he wasn't sure, but could only put it down to the strange circumstances.

"I...I want to apologize about earlier," she almost whispered, as she stared down at the ground. "Do you mind if I sit?"

Where were his manners? "Please do," he said, now standing until she was seated.

"My name is Olivia Foster. I live in Helena." She looked everywhere except at Joseph. "They mistook me for my...cousin twice removed, Cassandra Seymour – of *the* Seymour's."

Joseph raised his eyebrows. He had heard of the family. A high society family who were always in the news. It answered a lot of questions, except why she'd been mistaken for her cousin. It explained why she'd been kidnapped, though. He reached out his hand. "Joseph Davis, Bootmaker."

"I'm very pleased to meet you, Joseph Davis Bootmaker," she said, then chuckled. "I truly am grateful for your help this morning. I'm not sure where I would be now without you." She glanced down into her lap then. "My cousin Cassandra is an heiress, where I am merely her poor cousin. I'm not sure what would have happened had I not escaped."

Suddenly, Joseph felt awkward. *What did you say to someone who had been recently kidnapped?* Assuming her claim was true. "Would you like coffee? The diner's coffee is the best in town." Then it occurred to him. "How long since you've eaten?" *Why didn't he think of that before?*

"What day is it?" she asked, leaving him quite perplexed.

"Monday."

She closed her eyes and was suddenly thoughtful. "Friday I think. Or maybe Saturday. I'm not certain."

Joseph's heart thudded, and he stood. "Then let me buy you a meal." He reached for her hand to help Olivia to her feet. Her skin was soft, like a woman who had never done a day's work in her life. *Yet she said she was the poor cousin.*

"You don't have to…" she began, but he wanted to. Joseph felt strangely drawn to this woman who kept far more secrets than Joseph thought she probably should.

The meal was good. Joseph rarely indulged in lunch at the diner, but for Olivia's sake, he did so today. She had the chicken pot pie with vegetables, as well as chocolate cake for dessert. Joseph had the steak and apple pie for dessert. Not that she said a lot, but Olivia was good company. He avoided asking questions about her situation for fear she may run. It was the last thing he wanted, especially if she was in danger.

Surely the sheriff had asked crucial questions of her, anyway. "Where are you staying tonight?" It was one of the few questions he dared ask.

"The saloon, I guess."

Joseph was astounded. "I wouldn't suggest any woman stay there. It's not safe."

She stared at him curiously. "Where else can I stay? I've asked around, and it's the only place I've found."

He squirmed in his seat. *Dare he asked Tucker for this favor?* "Stay here, and I'll be back." He headed for Tucker and they chatted a few minutes, then he returned to their table. "Tucker is going to make enquiries on your behalf. He knows everyone in town and feels he can find temporary accommodation for you."

She appeared astonished. "He can do that?" Her voice was full of emotion.

"He is going to try. No guarantees, but he will make some enquiries and get back to me." When Joseph glanced up, Tucker was heading their way.

"Here's your coffee," he said as he placed two mugs on the table, along with a jug of cream.

Olivia glanced up at him. "Thank you," she said quietly. "For everything."

He smiled, then nodded. "Don't thank me yet. I have someone in mind, but will have to check with her first."

Joseph knew he spoke of Mrs. Baker, who previously owned the diner. She was a kind woman, and had helped young women in the past when they had nowhere to stay. He reached for his coffee. "You've got more color in your cheeks now. Does that mean you feel better?"

"I do. Thank you for everything. Everyone has been so kind, especially you." She smiled briefly at him, then glanced down at her lap.

Joseph felt sad for her. It seemed she was not used to kindness, which made him feel especially sad for her. "Kindness never hurt anyone," he said, then leaned over and covered her hand with his own. He had no idea why he did so. He wasn't one to be so forward, or so blatant. Especially with a stranger. But Olivia didn't feel like a stranger – she felt more like a long-lost friend. It felt as though they'd known each other forever. Joseph shook himself mentally.

This was absolutely ridiculous. More than likely, Olivia would be gone in a day or two. Her father would catch the stage or the train and come to Grand Falls and fetch her. The best thing he could do for both of them was to keep his distance. In the meantime, he would continue to enjoy the meal and conversation with this beautiful and very intriguing young woman.

He asked where she was from and questioned her about her family. Olivia seemed guarded, but he guessed a kidnap victim would be that way. Joseph was sure he would. "Do you have any siblings?"

She looked horrified at the question and stumbled through her answer. "I have…three older brothers and a sister. There are five of us in all."

Joseph raised an eyebrow. He knew little about the Helena Seymour's, but from what he remembered, there were five children. Olivia said she was the *poor cousin*.

Where were his thoughts taking him? He had no right to doubt what she told him. It wasn't like he could look the family up. Everything he knew about them he'd read in the newspapers. Even then, they were at least a week old when they arrived in Grand

Falls. It was pastime they had their own news press, in Joseph's opinion. Old news was no fun.

"Good afternoon." Joseph would know that voice anywhere.

"Mrs. Baker. Good afternoon to you." He motioned for her to sit, but knew the elderly woman would do whatever she wanted, anyway. "Allow me to introduce you to Miss Olivia Foster."

Mrs. Baker stared momentarily. "It's my pleasure," she said, then studied Olivia unbidden. It was all he could do not to chuckle. The older woman always did whatever she pleased, even if it was not acceptable in decent society. "You look familiar, my dear," she said, then turned to Joseph. "Leave us alone, Mr. Davis. I'd like to chat with Miss Foster."

He wasn't shocked at the request, and had, in fact, expected it. Mrs. Baker was a well-known identity in Grand Falls. "I must get back to work anyway," he said as he stood. "Can I order something for you, Mrs. Baker?"

"Just a coffee," she said, then waved him away. Joseph would love to listen in on the conversation, simply because Mrs. Baker often came out with the most inappropriate things. He'd had no chance to warn Olivia, as he didn't expect the older woman to appear so quickly. Well, nothing he could do about it now.

He said a quick goodbye, ordered the coffee, then paid the bill before returning to work.

~*~

"I know who you are," Mrs. Baker whispered, ensuring no one else in the diner heard her.

Olivia was horrified. "Please, don't…"

"I won't tell anyone. You can come and stay with me, and we can talk about it." She took a big gulp of coffee, then studied Olivia again. "You'll be safe at my cottage."

But will you? She dearly wanted to ask her new friend the question, but refrained. The last thing Olivia wanted was to put this dear lady in danger.

Olivia had no money; the kidnappers had taken the little money she carried. She was lucky to still have her reticule, not that it helped her much. Once the criminals had discovered exactly who she was, by going through her reticule, they had no use for her. She'd overheard them planning to *eliminate* her. Her heart thudded at the memory.

"Are you all right, my dear? You've gone quite pale." Olivia wasn't surprised. She might still be in shock, and who could blame her? She'd been through a lot over the past days, or was it a week? If she was honest with herself, Olivia had no idea of the passage of time. She didn't even know how she'd arrived at Grand Falls. She'd arrived on the train. She remembered that much, but beyond that, she did not know how she got here. There was a train ticket in her reticule, one that was issued in Hollow Valley, but she didn't know how she'd arrived there either. Or left there.

It would probably remain a mystery – one that might never be solved. The apothecary told her shock could cause memory loss, and apparently he was right.

Mrs. Baker stood. "Shall we go?" Olivia had finished her meal, and was truly grateful to Joseph Davis. It was then she realized she hadn't thanked him for the meal. Not in so many words. She made a mental note to do so later. She stood then, mimicking the kind-hearted woman standing before her. "I promise I don't bite," Mrs. Baker said with a chuckle.

It made Olivia laugh, probably for the first time in over a week. Or however long it had been since they took her against her will. The memory threatened to overtake her, and she felt light-headed. She grabbed the back of the chair for support, and out of the corner of her eye, she saw Mrs. Baker wave to someone in the diner. "Let's sit you down for a minute."

The male voice startled her, and she was about to scream when Mrs. Baker reassured her. "Everything is all right, Olivia. This is Tucker, the owner of the diner."

She let out the breath she'd been holding, and suddenly tears rolled down her face. Olivia was not one to cry, but so much had happened to her lately, and she couldn't take any more. She had endured ordeal after ordeal, and now she just wanted it to stop.

Tucker handed her a clean handkerchief. "Sit here and rest. I'll be back shortly," he whispered. She glanced up at him, but he didn't look worried or panicked, as so many men would be at a crying woman. He appeared calm and seemed to know what to do to make her feel better. He quickly reappeared with a mug of tea. "Sip that, and you'll feel better."

Olivia nodded and did what she was told. Tucker was right. She felt better. As she drank, she watched Mrs. Baker whisper something in Tucker's ear. He suddenly left the diner, but returned shortly afterwards with the bootmaker. Olivia's heart sank. She'd disturbed that poor man far more than she already should have.

"I'm sorry," she said quickly. "I'm fine now," and stood. The dizziness returned, and she almost fell back on the chair.

"Thank you for coming, Mr. Davis. It's the shock, you know," Mrs. Baker said quietly.

He studied her, his eyes filled with compassion, and Olivia almost cried again. She didn't want anyone to feel pity for her, let alone Joseph Davis.

"I'll be all right. I don't want to be a nuisance to anyone." If it wasn't so improper, Olivia would put her hands to her face and sob her heart out. But it wasn't something a young woman of her standing was supposed to do.

Joseph came to stand next to her, and his unique smell, mostly leather, filled her senses. "Just say when you're ready," he said gently.

She glanced up at him. "Ready for what?" She was confused and wasn't sure if her confusion was also from shock.

"Mr. Davis has agreed to join us, accompanying you to my cottage."

Olivia glanced from Mrs. Baker to Joseph. These people were far too kind, especially when she was a complete stranger to them both. "I've caused you both far too much misery already. I should wire my father to send money for the saloon."

"Phooey. I'll not have you stay at the saloon. It's not safe for any woman to be in that disgraceful place." Mrs. Baker leaned in close then. "I'm assuming you don't wish to become a soiled dove?"

Olivia opened her eyes in astonishment. *Was that really a possibility just by staying the saloon?* She'd led such a sheltered life, Olivia had no knowledge of such things. She shook her head vigorously, but that only made her light-headed again.

Tears welled in her eyes once more. "I feel like such a burden," she said on a sob.

Mrs. Baker was like the grandmother she'd never had and sat down beside Olivia. "You are not a burden. It gets very lonely at my cottage. I'm a widow, you know, so I live alone." She smiled then. "I tend to take in strays. Always young women who need support of some sort."

Olivia felt a little better then. At least she wasn't the only one. "I think I'm ready now."

Joseph held her arm and helped Olivia to her feet. Mrs. Baker stood on the other side of her. "Tucker would have come too, but he can't leave the diner unattended." Olivia nodded. She could understand that.

18

They were soon on their way to Mrs. Baker's cottage. Olivia hoped no harm would come to the kind-hearted woman for taking in someone who should have been dead already.

Olivia sipped her tea as Mrs. Baker studied her. "Fine mess you've got yourself into," her new friend said firmly. "We'll have to work out a plan."

Instead of answering, Olivia took another sip. "I'm concerned for Cassandra's safety. I don't know if she's safe, or if she has been taken now the kidnappers have realized I'm not who they thought I was." This time, she took a large gulp of the tea.

"Keep calm. Right now, you're safe. We can talk to the sheriff – he'll know what to do." Mrs. Baker stared at her over her mug of strong coffee. "In the meantime, you look tired. Why don't you take a nap?"

She had been fighting herself against sleep for over an hour, so perhaps Mrs. Baker was right. Olivia did not know how long it had been since she slept. She remembered nothing since before she boarded the train, so had no knowledge of when she last slept. She drank down the last of the tea, then stood. "Thank you for everything," she whispered. "I don't know where I would be right now if not for you."

"You have no need to thank me. I would do the same for anyone in need."

Olivia stepped toward the elderly woman, her head still in a fog. "Not everyone would do what you did," she said firmly. "We both know it." Mrs. Baker stood then, her own mug now empty. Olivia leaned in and hugged her. "I truly appreciate it," she whispered, then headed into the spare room.

Chapter Two

Three days later...

Joseph pounded the leather harder than he'd ever done before. He hadn't laid eyes on Olivia since he'd left her at Mrs. Baker's cottage. *Was the young woman all right? Was she even still in Grand Falls?*

He had absolutely no idea, and it was niggling away at him. For whatever reason, the answer to which he didn't know, he felt somehow responsible for Olivia Foster. Whether that was because he was the one to discover her wandering about unheeded, he had no idea. What he knew was his gut told him to look out for her.

With her hidden away in Mrs. Baker's cottage, there was little chance of that happening. Not that she would come to harm in the elderly woman's home. That certainly wasn't his concern. He simply wanted to know she was safe. The pity of it all was he spent the majority of his time in his workshop. He was not afforded a way to see out onto the street from there, so had no opportunity to notice strangers.

The good thing about Grand Falls was it was relatively small. Strangers stood out like a sore thumb. If anyone had been milling around, *someone* would have noticed. Not that they'd tell him necessarily, but more likely, the sheriff would find out. There was a rumor mill here that meant nothing was secret. There were a few town gossips, mostly elderly women who simply couldn't help themselves.

In this case, it was probably a good thing. If strangers had come to town, the sheriff would no doubt find out about it.

If it wasn't meant to be kept quiet, he could go into the mercantile and ask Cecil Delbert if any strangers had been asking questions about Olivia. Only he couldn't, because both Cecil and Hannah would want to know why he'd asked.

Instead, he put down his hammer, and went outside. The action was not out of place. Everyone in town had seen him do it from time to time. Being cooped up in his workroom was not good for him. One of these days, he might have windows installed – both front and back. That way, he would have natural light *and* a way to see what went on outside. His workroom had been designed to eliminate distractions, to ensure he did his job instead of watching the townsfolk.

He stepped out into the fresh air. Much as he had done that day he found Olivia wandering about.

Joseph stretched his arms and yawned. He felt better already.

Until he glanced toward the diner and saw two strangers about to enter the only decent eating place in town. His heart pounded. *Should he run to the sheriff? Or perhaps he should warn Olivia?* Either way, he knew it was fruitless. The men had done nothing the sheriff could deal with, and telling Olivia would likely scare her. Instead, he locked up his store and headed to the diner himself.

Since he rarely went to the diner, he needed a reason. He couldn't tell Tucker why he was there – the man would think him a fool. Instead, he decided to order coffee and a muffin. He deserved a treat for a change.

Joseph sat at the table way up the back, where he could easily watch the men without being obvious. He placed his order and glanced around. It wasn't busy yet, but he knew it would get like that soon. Tucker placed a lemon muffin in front of him, along with a mug of coffee. "We only have lemon muffins right now. Unless you want to wait for the new batch to come out of the oven."

Joseph took his eyes off the two men and glanced briefly at Tucker. "Lemon is fine. Thank you."

Tucker followed his line of sight, then sat down. "Any reason you are so interested in those two?"

"Wondering if they were Olivia's abductors," he whispered.

Instead of agreeing, Tucker laughed. "They're traveling salesmen. They come through town every few months. Surely you've seen them before?"

He shook his head. "Never," Joseph said. He felt embarrassed, but knew he should be happy at the outcome. It was another day Olivia was safe.

Without warning, Tucker stood. "Don't worry. I'm keeping an eye out." He turned toward the kitchen then, and Joseph began eating his muffin, enjoying every mouthful.

"I wish we knew what they looked like," Joseph said, more to himself than the retreating Tucker who turned back to face him.

"It would certainly help, but short of asking Olivia, there's no way to know."

Joseph nodded his agreement. Tucker was right; there really was only one way to find out, and that was to present himself at Mrs. Baker's cottage. *But would the old lady let him in?* It wasn't like he was a stranger – he'd lived in this town his entire life. Mrs. Baker had been here far longer than him.

He finished up his muffin and coffee, then left the diner. His belly was full, and he suddenly felt confident. Instead of returning to his store, he hurried to the cottage, which was on the outskirts of town. It wasn't far and wouldn't take long. He had no pressing orders, so he could afford the time.

Finally arriving, he took a long breath, then let it out slowly. Then he knocked on the door.

Out of the corner of his eye, Joseph saw the curtain being pulled aside. No doubt Mrs. Baker was checking who was at her door. She was always careful since she lived alone, but now, with Olivia there, she was being even more cautious.

The curtain fell aside and the door suddenly opened. "Mr. Davis! I'm surprised to see you here," the older woman said as she ushered him inside. He could see Olivia over her shoulder. She sat at the dining table drinking from a mug. "Sit down," Mrs. Baker said. "Let me get you some coffee."

She was gone before he had a chance to answer, so he did as he was told and sat at the table next to Olivia. It was the first time he'd seen her since he'd brought her here, and she looked far better. The dark circles under her eyes were gone, and her hair was right where it belonged instead of being disheveled as it was when he discovered her. "How are you feeling?"

She turned to face him and smiled tentatively. "Much better," she said quietly. "I can't thank you enough..."

He held up a hand. "No need for thanks. Any decent person would do what I did." At least he liked to think they would. He just happened to be in the right place at the right time. Even so, he couldn't, in all consciousness, have allowed her to proceed the way things were. It was like she was in some kind of trance, but of course, he now knew she was in shock. The mystery of it was she did not know how she arrived in this friendly town.

She reached out a hand and placed it on top of his. "Not everyone would help a complete stranger. I'll be forever grateful to you for your actions." He glanced down at her hand and was horrified at what he saw. There were ligature marks on her wrist that had previously been covered by the length of her sleeves, but as she stretched across to touch him, her sleeve moved further up her arm.

She followed his line of sight and quickly tugged at the wayward sleeve. "I…"

"You don't have to explain," he whispered. It was at that moment Mrs. Baker returned to the dining room. She glanced from one to the other, but didn't comment.

"Here you are Mr. Davis. Help yourself to a cookie." Mrs. Baker was an excellent cook, it's the reason the diner had been so popular for all those years. Now she had retired, after finding equally good people to replace her.

Joseph reached across the table, but knew he shouldn't. Especially after having already consumed a muffin today. He was not big on sweet foods, but he could be easily enticed. "This is delicious," he said appreciatively.

"So, Mr. Davis," his hostess said as she speared him with her gaze. "What can you tell us? Any strangers in town?"

He nodded, trying to fill in time while he swallowed down a mouthful of cookie. "I saw two men I'd never seen before, but Tucker said they're regular visitors to town. Travelers, he told me." There was a collective sigh of relief from the two women as he added the latter. "I'll continue to be vigilant," he said, taking another mouthful. When the cookie was gone, he swallowed down some coffee. "This is excellent coffee."

Mrs. Baker smiled. "I make the best coffee in town," she said firmly. "I've taught my successors, so the tradition will continue."

She was right. The coffee at the diner was as good as it ever was. Some things should never be changed. "I should probably be going." He began to stand, but Mrs. Baker did that thing she always did when she was displeased – she pierced him with a stare that could stop an army.

Joseph lowered himself back down. "I guess I could stay a little longer," he said, then took another sip of coffee. For a little old lady, she certainly got her own way.

"How is your business going, Mr. Davis? Busy?"

He lifted an eyebrow at her. "Steady, as always."

"I don't see a lot of you, and wondered if that meant you were too busy to visit a lonely old lady."

That made him chuckle. "I don't like to interfere," he said honestly. "There are times when I'm far too busy and under pressure, and others when I make boots to display."

"Your father taught you well."

Joseph drank down the last of his coffee. "I really must go now," he said, as once again he stood. "Is there anything I can do to help?"

"Let me know if you see any strangers in town. Or if you hear anything. Maybe chat to the sheriff – he might have some news."

Joseph knew if the sheriff had news, he would have passed it on to the women already, but agreed anyway. "Thank you for your hospitality," he said as he left.

Mrs. Baker stood at the door and waved goodbye. Joseph felt as though there were eyes on him as he left the cottage, but was certain he must have imagined it. He glanced about, and no one was in sight.

Chapter Three

Olivia knew it could be dangerous, but glanced out of the cottage window, regardless.

She watched as Mrs. Baker walked toward the main road and stopped to talk to people along the way. She needed supplies, the older woman had said, and Olivia didn't doubt her. Suddenly her breath hitched – Sheriff Saxon delayed her, asking many questions. At least, that's what Olivia thought. By this stage, Mrs. Baker was far from the cottage, and it was difficult to truly know what was happening.

Suddenly Mrs. Baker threw her hands in the air, then stormed off from the lawman and into the mercantile. Had he guessed the truth? Olivia hoped not. Mrs. Baker thought if they could keep her true identity secret for at least a few days longer, but hopefully more, the danger would pass.

Olivia wasn't as confident as her hostess. What she'd come to understand in the short time she'd been hidden away was nothing got passed her elder. Mrs. Baker might come across as an old lady who kept mostly to herself, but Olivia knew better. From the moment they'd met, she'd known who Olivia was and offered to conceal her. It was far more than she could or would ask for, but she was also eternally grateful to the caring woman.

They'd sat for hours, drinking coffee and chatting. She'd convinced Olivia to tell her the whole sordid story, despite her reluctance. Her tears had flowed as she'd recited what had occurred, from the moment she'd been snatched, until she'd escaped. After that, she couldn't recall. Her last memory was of her kidnappers discussing how to *get rid of her*, since she was not who they thought she was.

Olivia swallowed. If not her, it would have been Cassandra…she couldn't bear to think about it. For either of them, it was a bitter pill to swallow. She knew Richard Seymour, her father, would pay a ransom, no matter the price, and no matter which daughter. As far as she could tell, no ransom had been demanded while she was in their possession. *What did those kidnappers really want?*

It was baffling, not only to Olivia, but to Mrs. Baker as well.

The front door rattled, and she was frozen in fear. *Had they found her?* Olivia had spent most of her time daydreaming. Well, not daydreaming exactly. She had been mulling over the events of the past week or so. Suddenly, the door pushed open and Mrs. Baker stepped inside. Olivia was light-headed with relief.

"Are you all right, my dear?"

Olivia rushed to take the large box out of the tiny woman's hands. "I should have come with you," she said. "This box is far too heavy for you. Besides, I'm sure they would have delivered it." It was more of a statement than a question, and Olivia carried the box into the small kitchen.

Mrs. Baker raised an eyebrow. "And risk someone discovering you here?" She reached into the box and tossed a newspaper Olivia's way. Her heart pounded and terror filled her as she slowly opened the folded paper.

Heiress Kidnapped. All Hope Lost

Her hands went to her throat. "My father must be desperate." Tears rolled down her pale face. Mrs. Baker reached out and took her hands.

"The sheriff has worked it all out. He accosted me on my way to the mercantile."

"I'm sorry, Mrs. Baker. I have caused you far too much trouble already." She wiped the tears from her face and headed toward the front door.

"Where are you going?" Mrs. Baker's voice was calm. It made Olivia feel less agitated.

"To speak to the sheriff. There's no point hiding it, if it's all over town already." Her heart sank. She realized that also meant Joseph Davis knew the truth, too. The man had been so kind to her. Not only had he arranged medical treatment when she needed it, but had fed her as well. Not to mention escorting her to this quaint little cottage where she now stood.

"He'll be here sometime this afternoon. In the meantime, we should make lunch." Mrs. Baker busied herself unpacking the box and putting everything away. "How do you feel about pancakes with potatoes and onion? I'd make vegetable soup, but it takes too long to cook. Perhaps we can have that tonight."

Olivia sighed. If the sheriff was visiting later that day, she might not still be there for this evening's meal. "He'll lock me up in the jail for impersonating someone else." She glanced down and noticed her hands were visibly shaking.

Mrs. Baker laughed. "He's more concerned with keeping you safe. Here, help me with this." She indicated for Olivia to open a cupboard that was a little high for the other woman to reach. "I don't normally cook pancakes for myself." Olivia knew the other woman had owned the diner for many years and was an excellent cook. She also knew she'd been a widow for a very long time. "This will be a treat for me." She glanced across at Olivia. "And you too, I hope." She smiled then and Olivia suddenly felt better.

There was a knock at the door. Mrs. Baker glanced up. "It's too early for the sheriff. Hide in the bedroom. Climb out the window if things go awry."

Olivia's hands went to her mouth in shock. "I could never leave you alone if there was trouble. You've been so kind."

Mrs. Baker glared at her. "I'm an old lady nearing the end of my life. You are young. Do what I say." She was determined, Olivia would give her that, but she would not comply. Not under any circumstances.

Olivia hurried to the front door and pulled it open before Mrs. Baker could interfere. "Joseph!" It was such a relief to see a friendly face. Only he didn't look friendly at that moment. He had a fierce expression on his face.

"I'm Joseph, but who are you? Not the cousin of the Seymour's, that's for sure."

She shook her head sadly. "No, I'm not. I am the second daughter of Richard Seymour. By far, the richest man in Helena."

You could have almost picked Joseph up off the ground. He knew there was something not quite right with Olivia, but wasn't certain what it was. "You're an heiress?" His head was spinning. This was not a development he'd foreseen. She didn't come across as someone used to high society, but he was certain there was something amiss.

Olivia shrugged her shoulder. An action he wouldn't expect a woman of her position in elite society to do. "According to my father, I'm the wild child. It's probably the reason he kept my kidnapping quiet." She turned away then, and Joseph suspected it was to stop him from seeing her tears. But she turned to late. He'd seen them for only a split second, but long enough to notice her distress.

He moved toward her and pulled Olivia close. Joseph wrapped his arms around her and caressed her back. How he wished to protect her from all her worries. He longed to hold her like this forever. It wasn't long before she let herself relax against him and then sobbed. "What am I going to do? Those men...I've seen them here in town."

He stared down at her and brushed away the tears. "You've seen them here? You didn't...why didn't you say something?"

"The sheriff knows." Her arms slipped up around his waist, and she gripped him like she would never let go. It wasn't that Joseph was unhappy, but he knew the longer it happened, the harder it would be to let her go.

His arms tightened, despite needing to do the opposite. He stared across the room toward the window. Two men could be seen through the curtains. Mrs. Baker ran to the sitting room and pulled down the blind.

"Is that them?" he asked. Olivia nodded. At least he knew what they looked like now. Not that he could do much about it. But he had to protect these women. Besides, two against one wouldn't help anyone.

"I was about to make lunch, Mr. Davis. Consider yourself invited."

He nodded. It wasn't in his plans, but no way was Joseph leaving now. "I appreciate it. What can I do to help?"

Mrs. Baker considered him. "You can do what you're already doing – comforting Olivia, and making me feel safe."

In all his days, he'd never known the older woman to admit she didn't feel safe. Nor had he known her to rely on others. She was a strong woman. She'd had to be once her husband had died. Not that Joseph had the pleasure of meeting him, but Henry Baker was said to be a pillar of society.

"The trouble is," Olivia said. "According to the sheriff, he has no cause to arrest those men. Unless they try to grab me again, he can't touch them. They've broken no laws in Grand Falls." She glanced up at him. "It's my word against theirs."

Joseph knew what the sheriff said was true, but there had to be a way to keep her safe. And the only way to do that was to have the men jailed. There had to be a way to achieve that, but what it was, he was yet to discover.

What was required, at least in Joseph's mind, was a plan of some sort to entice those men to break the law. But didn't that also make him implicit? No matter what happened, the aim was to keep Olivia safe.

When he glanced across, it was clear Olivia was on the verge of tears again. She fought them gallantly, probably for his sake, but it was the last thing Joseph wanted. He strode to her side and took her in his arms. It was the worst thing he could have done.

The moment he wrapped her in his arms, tears fell down her face. He rubbed his hands in circles, trying to comfort her. He was almost certain he'd comforted her, but he also felt himself being drawn to her. Not that he hadn't been already. The moment he set eyes on this damsel in distress, he'd felt a connection with her. Now that he'd held her so intimately, it felt even more so.

He pulled a clean handkerchief from his pocket and handed it to her. "I...I'm sorry," she whispered. "I didn't mean to fall to pieces." She began to pull away, but Joseph held her firmly in place.

"You have every right to feel that way," he said. "I can't even imagine what you've endured." He glanced down at her then. Her face was still crumpled in anguish. He leaned down and gently kissed her forehead.

He had shocked himself. Joseph barely knew this woman, and yet he'd taken liberties by kissing her. No, it wasn't on her lips, even so, it was an intimate move, and one he had no right to do. He straightened and noticed Mrs. Baker standing there, watching him. A small smile tugged at her lips.

He was devastated and yet she seemed pleased. *What was wrong with the woman?* She was known for her matchmaking endeavors, but this was nothing to do with love. This was all about comforting a distressed woman.

"Perhaps a nice cup of tea would help? What do you think, Olivia?" She pulled back from him and nodded her agreement. "Coffee, Mr. Davis?"

"Thank you," he said quietly. "I have no intention of leaving you ladies alone. While ever those criminals are hanging about, I will be here for protection."

Mrs. Baker stared at him. "I have my Henry's handgun in the bedroom. I'll get it for you." She hurried away and returned with the gun, handing it over. "It's not loaded," she said, then gave him a box of bullets. "Let's hope it's not required." Her lips were pulled into a tight line, and it was the first sign Joseph had seen of worry from the widow.

Joseph went to the window and pulled the curtain slightly aside. "I think they're gone," he said. "Or they could still be hanging about and want us to think that." He let the curtain fall back into place. He shuddered at the thought of the gun in his hands. It wasn't that he didn't know how to use one, because he did. His father had taught him to shoot to hunt, when he was a mere child. They'd hunted regularly, until his father had died. It wasn't Joseph's favorite thing to do, but he was now grateful that he knew how to handle a gun correctly, and could protect the two sweet women in his care.

He opened the box and loaded bullets into the chamber. "You look like you know what you're doing," Mrs. Baker said, then sighed as though with relief.

"It's been a while, but yes. I used to hunt with my father. Of course, we used rifles, and not handguns. Still, I feel confident enough to protect you ladies." He glanced across at Olivia and saw fear covered her face. He put the gun down and went to her side. "Everything will be all right." He put an arm around her, and it felt familiar, as though he'd done it a thousand times before.

She glanced up and gingerly smiled. The smile didn't reach her eyes, and it was clear to Joseph she was trying to put on a brave face. He felt her shudder under his touch, and he worried for her.

He'd been drawn in to this ring of danger, but he was not afraid for himself. Mrs. Baker was an innocent bystander who had accepted the risk of protecting the younger woman, and that was exactly the way he felt.

Banging on the front door startled him, and Olivia let out a shriek. "You ladies go to the kitchen," he commanded, then snatched up the gun. Joseph cautiously strode to the door and quickly opened it, gun at the ready.

"Joseph!" the sheriff said. "What are you doing here?"

He let out a sigh of relief. "Sheriff! I'm very pleased to see you." He ushered the sheriff inside, then locked the door behind him. "It's safe to come out, ladies."

"Sheriff," Mrs. Baker said. "The kidnappers have been here."

Sheriff Earl Saxon scowled. "When was this?"

"Only minutes ago," Joseph said. "You must have practically crossed paths with them."

"I didn't see anyone I didn't already know," he said firmly. Despite his words, he went to the window and peeked behind the curtains. "No one is there now."

Of course not, Joseph decided. They would take off when they saw the sheriff heading their way. He sighed. "They most definitely were. I'm staying as long as it takes. These ladies need protection."

"If you're sure?" Sheriff Saxon seemed dubious, but Joseph had made a promise to protect Olivia and Mrs. Baker, and that was exactly what he would do.

"If they can put up with me, I'll be here twenty-four hours a day until the danger has passed." He glanced across to Mrs. Baker, who nodded her acceptance.

"You can sleep on the couch," she said. "If you can fit," she added as she sized him up. "I have plenty of spare blankets."

"Don't you worry about me. I can always make a pallet on the floor."

"You're every bit as tall as I remember your dear father being," Mrs. Baker said, melancholy coming through in her voice. "He was such a wonderful man. I remember both of your parents well."

Wonderful memories hit Joseph without warning, but as much as he loved and missed both his parents, he needed to keep his focus.

"Well, you clearly don't need my help, so I'll be on my way. I'll check in from time to time and make sure you're all fine." He donned his hat, then left without another word. Joseph glanced out the door before closing it, then returned to the dining table.

When he studied Olivia, she looked none too pleased. "Are you all right, Olivia?" She nodded, but he wasn't convinced.

"This is all too much. Not only do I have to worry about kidnappers trying to abduct me again, but now I've caused you to abandon your business for goodness knows how long." Tears welled in her eyes, and Joseph watched as she fought them back.

He reached across the table and patted her hand. "Don't worry about me," he said gently. "I have no pending orders, and all I'm doing right now is filling the display shelves."

He felt Mrs. Baker's eyes on him and glanced up. Once again, she was fighting back a smile. The last thing Joseph wanted or needed was to become involved with a woman on the run. He was not interested in marriage, but especially to someone who came with the difficulties Olivia possessed.

He shook himself mentally. Why was he even thinking like this? Of course he knew – it was Mrs. Baker's influence. The darned woman did this all the time to eligible bachelors. She liked to pair off unsuspecting couples and then ensured they got together and eventually married. They might have been well suited, but she was influential enough that couples rarely fought back. Well, that wouldn't be the case here. Joseph had no intention of marrying, nor did he intend to court anyone, and especially not Olivia. She was far too complicated for him.

"I need to start supper," Mrs. Baker said, bringing him out of his wayward thoughts. Joseph tucked the gun into his pants, then went to the window, again checking all was fine outside. He was certain it was an action he would repeat often until the kidnappers were caught.

Olivia had moved to the couch, and he sat down next to her. "Why did you hide your true identity?" he asked, trying to hide the hurt, but failing miserably.

She turned to face him. "I thought it would be safer. If you thought I was the poor cousin, you might not fuss over me so much."

Joseph cringed. Would he even think that way? He truly wasn't sure. "Well, it didn't work." He chuckled then, and it made her smile briefly. She was so beautiful when she smiled, despite the scratches on her face. He reached up and touched them, caressing her soft skin as though his ministrations would heal her sorrow.

When he realized what he was doing, he quickly pulled his hand back. Their eyes locked, and Joseph could not pull his gaze away. Instead, they sat staring at each other for what seemed forever.

Until Mrs. Baker came back into the room and cleared her throat. "Is there anything you don't eat, Mr. Davis?" She sounded irritated, and he couldn't fathom why. She seemed to be pushing them together, but at the same time annoyed with his actions.

He turned to face her. "I'll eat anything," he said. Mrs. Baker seemed like her normal self again, making him believe he'd misunderstood her mood.

"I've made fresh coffee if you're up for another? I have biscuits in the oven as well." They say the way to a man's heart is through his belly, and they are right. Joseph certainly liked his food.

Chapter Four

Joseph awoke to kitchen clatter. He had slept well given the circumstances, and placed himself in front of the fire, which wasn't far from the front door. If anyone had broken in that way, he would be the first to know.

He reached in under the pillow for the gun Mrs. Baker had given him, to assure himself it was still there.

Mrs. Baker was a gracious hostess, not that he was surprised. He'd not had a lot of contact with her over the years, and what he had was scant. Joseph wasn't a social person and rarely attended any of the town events.

It wasn't that he didn't like people, it was more that he didn't really know most of the locals. Sure, he knew them to say hello, or to check how they were doing, but that was about it. He knew Tucker because they were around the same age and had attended school together. Of course, he knew the owners of the mercantile, and a few other store owners. But beyond that, he was almost a stranger to everyone else.

After church, he went straight home. When he thought about it, his parents weren't much different. Mother was always in a rush to leave so she could check on the roast she had cooking while they attended the Sunday service. They didn't socialize a lot, and it made perfect sense that Joseph had turned out the same way.

"Coffee is on the table, Mr. Davis. Breakfast will be ready shortly." Mrs. Baker made sure he was properly awake before she served up his meal. The aroma coming from that kitchen was more than a little enticing.

"Thank you," he called. He took a quick trip to the necessary and was back in record time. "This is delicious," he said, taking a mouthful after they'd said grace. He glanced across at Olivia and reveled in the way she looked this soon after she'd awoken. Her hair was hanging down her back, and not pulled back in a severe bun as it normally was. Her slumberous appearance was quite appealing, and he wouldn't be unhappy to wake up to such a beautiful sight every morning.

Joseph halted his thoughts right there. He had no wish to marry Olivia, or anyone for that matter, which was the only way he would get to see Olivia this way each morning. Apart from now, while he was protecting her, that was. "Good morning," he said quietly, realizing he hadn't greeted her already.

"Did you sleep well?" Even her voice sounded half asleep. It was rather endearing.

Joseph knew he had to find a way to keep his distance from the alluring Olivia Foster. Er, Seymour. He was the last person somebody of her standing would be interested in. But he wasn't interested in anyone, and that was the way he wanted it to stay.

"How is your food, Mr. Davis?"

Mrs. Baker stared at him curiously. "It's delicious, thank you. I normally skip breakfast."

Now she appeared exasperated. "Not while you're under my roof. Breakfast is the most important meal of the day. It's the reason I always offered breakfast at the diner."

He knew that to be true. The dear lady ran herself into the ground to accommodate those who required a hot meal in the mornings. "I can't…"

"be bothered. Most single men are the same. That's why you need to marry, and soon," she said firmly. When Mrs. Baker took to an idea, she insisted it came to fruition. *That wasn't so bad when it applied to other people, but when she made him her pet project?* That was not a suitable position to be in.

He shook himself mentally. "You're probably right. It's no fun to cook for one." A slow smile crossed her face, and Joseph knew he'd played right into her hands.

"Do you cook, Olivia?"

The young woman appeared startled. "I'm afraid not."

"Well!" Mrs. Baker huffed. "I shall have to teach you. All young women should learn to cook, no matter their social standing." She reached for her tea, and took large gulps as if trying to wash away her disgust.

"Thank you, Mrs. Baker," the younger woman said.

Joseph smiled briefly at Olivia, and his smile was returned. For all he knew, Olivia wanted to learn to cook. One day she might marry, and her husband may not be in the same league as her father. Deep down, he knew that wouldn't happen. The Seymour's of Helena were filthy rich. There was no way they would let any of their daughters marry outside their own social standing.

Not that Joseph was interested. Oh no, that was not his scene. He liked the quiet life, the simple life, and that's exactly why he lived in Grand Falls. He could have left anytime he'd wanted. Especially after he'd lost his parents. He loved the life he lived here and wasn't interested in leaving.

He'd had offers to move his business to larger towns, but that didn't interest him at all. Money wasn't everything, despite being how it was presented to him. Living a life with meaning – that was more his style. He wasn't rich, but he wasn't poor either. He made enough to live on, and then some. He didn't have to rush about like they did in the city, and he could take his own time with his work.

Mrs. Baker shoved a plate of biscuits toward him. "Have some more, Mr. Davis."

Joseph patted his belly. "I've eaten far more for breakfast than I usually have, even over several days."

"Huh! I knew you weren't eating properly," she said, glaring at him. "A wife would fix that. She would ensure you ate properly."

He felt like screaming *enough already. I don't want to get married!* However, Joseph was far too polite to do that to his friendly hostess. Her smirk told him she knew that would be it case. It wasn't that Olivia didn't appeal to him, because she did. But she was totally out of his reach. The more he thought about it, the more endeared he felt toward her. Each time his thoughts wandered that way, he had to convince himself not to think about it.

Besides, she wasn't from around here. A woman with her upbringing wouldn't even consider living in a small town like this. She had enjoyed the high life; going to the theater, dances, regattas – Grand Falls had none of those things. The closest they had were the monthly church dances. They would be tiny in comparison, and were held in the church hall, not in some fancy ballroom with ladies wearing their finest. In Helena, their finest would cost a pretty penny, whereas here, a woman's finest would be her Sunday best.

No, Olivia wasn't the sort of woman who would be interested in living in Grand Falls, let alone have any sort of endearment for a mere bootmaker.

"More coffee, Mr. Davis?" Mrs. Baker stood at his side, his plate in one hand, and the coffeepot in the other. A smirk crossed her face. It was as though she knew exactly what he was thinking, and in Joseph's mind, it was all the cunning old woman's fault.

He put his hand across the top of his mug. "I'm full to the point of bursting. I couldn't drink another drop. But thank you." *Was he imagining it, or did Mrs. Baker look as though she would burst out laughing at any moment?*

"Totally your choice," she said, then wandered into the kitchen, the coffeepot still in her hand. She looked totally at home in the kitchen, and he was convinced it was all those years running the diner. How on earth she'd managed it alone, he did not know. Sporadically she had help, but she was alone more often than she had any help.

He shook his head. The woman was amazing. Her husband, Henry, had died many years earlier. Joseph remembered him well. He was a pillar of society, just as Mrs. Baker was. The entire town had changed after his death. Everyone in Grand Falls mourned the death of Henry Baker. Many still did. The worst of it was Mrs. Baker had continued to run the diner without him. It wasn't until recently, she'd handed the diner's ownership over to Maggie and Tucker Smith. Mrs. Baker was in her late seventies now, and he wasn't the only person in Grand Falls relieved when that happened. She deserved a break, to retire and enjoy the rest of her life.

He glanced around the cottage. He remembered when it was built. Of course, he was only a teenager when that happened. Sawdust Harry built it, and still builds houses here in town. At least now he's not working alone since Patrick Harper came to town. Grand Falls was growing, and Joseph hoped and prayed it didn't grow to be anywhere near as big as Helena. To Joseph's mind, it was perfect just the way it was.

Dishes rattled in the kitchen, and the scraping of Olivia's chair brought him out of his daydreams. He seemed to do a lot of that lately. Joseph was convinced it was because he was doing nothing. Idle hands meant far too much time to think. That's what his father always told him, and Joseph was certain he was right. He was never melancholy when he was working, so this was something new for him.

"Mr. Davis!" Mrs. Baker called to him from the kitchen. *Was she in danger?* He shoved his chair back, making a terrible scraping noise, then hurried into the other room. "Oh, there you are," she said, shoving a kitchen cloth into his hands.

Joseph stared at her. "I thought there was some sort of problem," he said, feeling somewhat annoyed. "You sounded desperate."

She chuckled then. "I am – desperate for someone to dry the dishes. Olivia is clearing the table, so that left you. Hurry up then. I'm running out of space."

He couldn't help but chuckle. Mrs. Baker was a manipulator from way back, and nothing had changed.

With all the dishes washed and dried, he helped put them away, under instruction from Mrs. Baker. Olivia sauntered into the room with the soiled table cloth, as well as the sugar bowl and salt and pepper shakers. "I'll get started on supper," Mrs. Baker said. "Olivia, if you feel up to it, this can be your first cooking lesson." She raised her eyebrows at the young woman, who merely nodded her head.

The older woman pulled out a large cooking pot and placed it on the stove. She cut up meat and braised it, then added some water to the pot. It reminded Joseph of watching his mother cook. He felt out of place in here. He stood about doing nothing, which went against the grain. "Do you need my help in here?" he asked. When he was waved aside, he went back to the dining room and added more logs to the fire. It wasn't freezing, but the early morning air had a distinct chill to it. At least he felt as though he was being helpful. He detested standing around doing nothing; Joseph preferred being productive even if that was only to fuel the fire.

The thought made him glance across at the wood pile. It was getting low, so he'd need to refill it. He hadn't cut wood for some time, but he was certain he could still manage it without cutting off a limb. *What sort of protector would he be with a hand or arm missing?* The thought made him chuckle.

"I'll go out and cut some wood for you, Mrs. Baker."

She turned and glanced at him. "No need. I have already arranged for a delivery of cut wood. It should arrive later today." She turned back then and continued with her supper preparation.

He should have known. Mrs. Baker had lived alone for many years and would have a routine. She likely had a delivery arranged for a certain time every month. She had always been organized – she had to be that way to run the diner alone. "What can I do to help you?" he said, feeling fidgety. Joseph was not used to being idle.

"Keep an eye out for those kidnappers. I trust you still have Henry's gun close at hand."

Joseph felt about his waist. His heart pounded, and he sprinted into the dining room. It lay on the table where he'd left it during breakfast, only now it was on the bare table, and not on top of the table cloth where it had been.

Olivia must have moved it when she clear the table earlier. He could only imagine how she must have felt having to remove such a ghastly item. He would have to ensure he wasn't so careless from now on. It could mean the difference between life and death for these women. Not to mention himself.

He shoved the gun into his waist, then went to the window. He dragged the curtains back, but saw no one except for a few customers heading into the mercantile. Sheriff Saxon wandered about, glancing here and there, then heading toward the cottage. No doubt looking for the kidnappers, and ensuring they weren't around. He let the curtain drop as slowly as he'd opened it. The last thing he wanted was for someone to notice the action. Especially the kidnappers.

There was a knock at the door. He heard the gasp from within the kitchen. "It's all right," he called over his shoulder. "It's Sheriff Saxon." He carefully opened the door to ensure it was the sheriff, as he'd believed. "Come on in, Sheriff," he said, opening the door wider. "The ladies are in the kitchen."

The sheriff removed his hat, placing it on the hat stand that stood inside the door. "Good morning ladies."

"Good morning, Sheriff," Mrs. Baker answered. "Care for some coffee?" The woman must have an endless supply of coffee, Joseph decided. Likely a throwback from owning the diner.

"I wouldn't say no," he said, then took the steaming mug she handed to him only moments later.

"Sit yourself down in the sitting room," she said. "I'll be out in a moment." She handed Joseph a mug as well, and the two men did what they were told.

"There's no sign of any strangers being around," the sheriff said once they were all in the sitting room. Mrs. Baker offered each man a cookie. Joseph declined, but the sheriff accepted the offer. "These are delicious," he said, then took another mouthful. "I can't say for sure, but it appears to be safe for Miss Seymour to leave the cottage if she wants."

"She doesn't want," Mrs. Baker said firmly. "How do you know they're not hiding when they see you about?"

The sheriff swallowed down another mouthful of coffee. "The truth is, I don't. I have no proof they are even here."

"But I saw them!" Olivia screeched, near hysterical. "They *are* here." Tears began to fill her eyes, but she fought valiantly. Joseph wanted to go to her, to offer her comfort, but he also didn't want the sheriff to misunderstand his intentions. When her tears fell, he could hold back no longer. He hurried across to her and held her close. "I'm sorry," she whispered, but he hushed her apology.

"Don't be sorry," he whispered back. "You must be terrified."

She glanced up at him then. "Not with you protecting me." He leaned in and kissed her forehead, his hands moving in circles across her back. Something in him shifted, but Joseph wasn't sure what it was. What he knew was that things would never be the same for him again.

Olivia dried her eyes and silently admonished herself for falling apart. Especially in front of the two men. Breaking down in front of Mrs. Baker wasn't so bad, but to do so in front of men, that was unforgivable.

The situation she found herself in was incredibly intense, and she knew that was the cause of her distress, but her upbringing did not allow for tears unless one was alone. It was an indulgence she was not afforded.

But standing here now, wrapped in the arms of her self-appointed protector? It didn't feel like an indulgence. It felt as though she mattered to someone. Back home, it was as though she was merely a chattel, something that belonged to her father. She wasn't a real person to him – at least that's what it felt like. Her existence was merely tolerated, and that same thing applied to her sister Cassandra.

Her brothers were entirely different. They were important to the family name and the family business. They would continue the Seymour legacy long after their father was gone. *But the girls?* They would be married off to men of equal standing, and he could wash his hands of them. At least, that's what it felt like to Olivia.

Joseph glanced down at her, and she felt reassured. For the first time since she was kidnapped, Olivia felt as though everything could turn out all right. She felt his hand on her back, and he pulled her a little closer. Her heart rate accelerated.

"I'm doing what I can," she heard the sheriff say. "As little as that is. Even if I find them, there's not a lot I can do."

Olivia straightened her back. *Nothing he could do? He was joking, surely?* Those men kidnapped her right off the streets of Helena, held her hostage for days on end, and threatened to murder her. But he could do nothing.

She had never felt so angry in her life. "So Sheriff," she said, pulling away from Joseph. "You are saying my word is worth nothing. Perhaps I should message my father and let him deal with this from now on. I'm sure he would be happy to get the marshals involved."

Olivia watched as the sheriff stiffened. While she sounded very self-assured, she trembled inside. Joseph's hand caressed her cheek, and he glanced down at her. He leaned in close and whispered. "You're shaking," then pulled her close once again. She rested her head against his shoulder and reveled in his strength. Her eyes didn't leave the sheriff, not for even a moment. She glanced across at Mrs. Baker, who was grinning from ear to ear. At least Olivia knew she had the older woman's approval.

Sheriff Saxon walked over to the window and peeked from behind the curtains. "There are no strangers to be seen," he said, as though affirming his authority, then strolled to the door. "I'll keep in touch, but I think your *kidnappers* are long gone." In the blink of an eye, *he* was gone.

"That man," Olivia began, but Joseph soothed her temper.

"We know what happened to you, and believe every word you said. He has no proof, and that's his problem. Perhaps it would be worthwhile contacting your father. I'm sure he's worried sick."

Her heart thudded. Of course, Joseph was right. It's something she should have done already. He also needed to protect Cassandra. She stiffened again. At the very least, she may have put her older sister in danger. Once more, her tears fell unbidden. Joseph's arms wrapped around her were comforting, but wouldn't fix the situation she found herself in.

"Give me the details, and I'll message your father." He tipped her head up, so she faced him. His eyes were gentle, and she'd never seen such caring in a man's face before. All those men her father had lined up for her to marry – they were gold-diggers and nothing more. Father had promised a generous dowry. Joseph was the opposite; he was genuinely worried about her, Olivia the person, not the daughter of the richest man in Helena.

Mrs. Baker was clattering about in the kitchen again, and suddenly reappeared. "I've made you a mug of tea, coffee for you, Mr. Davis," she said. "The nerve of the man, intimating Olivia had made the entire thing up. She put down the mugs, almost slammed them down, then came closer, rubbing a hand up Olivia's arm. "I'm very proud of you standing your ground." She turned then and left them alone.

As much as she knew her father would do whatever it took, she wasn't convinced she should contact him yet.

Mrs. Baker glanced out the window. Another day had passed, and Joseph had spent another night on the pallet in the dining room. It pained Olivia he was suffering discomfort because of her, not to mention his business would be hurting.

"Good morning, Mr. Davis."

If he wasn't awake before, he certainly would be now. Mrs. Baker's voice was almost at bellowing level, even when she didn't mean it to be. That was likely a result of having to talk over the chatter at the diner for so long.

He half sat and wiped at his eyes. "Is it really morning already?" Olivia watched as he unfurled himself to a standing position. He was wearing the same clothes he'd worn since he arrived. He must surely feel uncomfortable. Olivia was lucky that Mrs. Baker arranged the mercantile to deliver clothes for her, otherwise she'd be in the same position.

"Breakfast is almost ready." Mrs. Baker had a way of giving him the hurry-up without actually saying it. He was suddenly far more alert. "After breakfast, I suggest you go home and change into fresh clothes. Clean yourself up a little."

He stared at her momentarily. "Of course."

"I feel bad you've been stuck here. I'm sure it's safe now." Olivia wasn't as sure as she sounded, but she didn't want to impose on him any further.

Joseph stared at her, his expression incredible. "That's not going to happen," he said firmly. "I will take Mrs. Baker's advise and then return."

"Not until after breakfast you won't," their hostess said firmly. "I went to a lot of trouble to make these pancakes."

Despite the situation, Olivia couldn't help but chuckle. The dear lady appeared quite affronted, and Joseph looked confused. She pulled out a chair for him and guided Joseph into the chair. The two women stared down at him, chuckling. In reality, Olivia knew it was no laughing matter. It only went to prove the dear man was lacking sleep. Not that she knew him well, but he appeared quite out of sorts today.

The ladies both sat and grace was said, then Mrs. Baker piled his plate with pancakes. Joseph stared down at them and then tucked in. The man certainly did like his food. What he would do after this ordeal was over, she had no idea.

Chapter Five

Joseph heard a scuffle outside and decided to check what was going on. A group of men headed toward Mrs. Baker's cottage.

It had been some days since the telegraph had been sent to Olivia's father, and since the group was headed up by Sheriff Saxon, he could only assume this group were protectors sent by Richard Seymour, Olivia's father.

Pounding on the door began before he had a chance to open it. "Where's my daughter?" The scowl on the man's face told Joseph this was her father, and he was none too pleased about the situation his daughter was in. He glanced over Joseph's shoulder and glared. *Was he offended by the cottage? Surely a father would be more concerned about his daughter's welfare than the size of the cottage she'd been kept in for her own protection?*

"Father?" Olivia's voice could be heard from the guest bedroom. Four men stood somberly behind him, and Joseph assumed they were either marshals or Pinkertons. Either way, they'd been brought there to protect Olivia.

"Olivia!" he said, wrapping his arms around his daughter. "I'm so glad to see you." He held her tight, and didn't let go for what seemed a lifetime.

His daughter glanced up at him and licked her lips. "Is…tell me Cassandra is safe?"

Her father smiled. "She is well protected." Olivia sighed with relief.

"This is Joseph Davis," she said when she finally pushed away. Her father glared at him, and Joseph totally understood. "He's been protecting me, Father. He doesn't deserve your wrath."

Reluctantly, Richard Seymour offered his hand. "Thank you, son," he said gruffly. "I appreciate your help, but as you can see, I've brought bodyguards to look after my little girl."

Joseph nodded. As much as he was relieved to know Olivia would be safe, he was going to miss her. Mrs. Baker too, despite the older woman's often difficult ways.

"This is Mrs. Baker," Olivia told her father, as her hostess entered the room. "This is her home. She graciously offered me refuge here."

"Pleased to meet you, Mr. Seymour. I'm pleased to see you have everything covered." It was obvious to Joseph that Olivia's father disapproved of the homely cottage, but without it, his daughter would not have been safe.

Ever the hostess, Mrs. Baker offered them all coffee and cookies. Seeing all those burly men sitting around the small dining table was almost laughable, but Joseph kept his wits about him and fought the urge to chuckle. As though she read his thoughts, Olivia flashed him a fleeting smile.

"Tell me about these kidnappers," her father said when they were all settled with coffee.

Sheriff Saxon had sat quietly until then. "I've seen no strangers in town, and have no proof of a kidnapping."

All eyes turned to him. "Are you calling my daughter a liar?" Richard Seymour asked quietly. Despite the gentle tone he used, the question came across as menacing. This was definitely a man who was used to getting his way and knew how to manipulate people to get what he wanted.

Heat moved up the sheriff's face, from his neck right up to the top of his head, but he stood his ground. "Of course not," he blurted out. "It's just…"

"It doesn't matter what you think. She knows what happened and my daughter doesn't lie. These men will look after her."

The sheriff took a long draw on his coffee, emptying the mug, then pushed back his chair. "If you don't need me, I'll be on my way." The room was silent, and he left without further ado. Joseph felt sorry for the sheriff, but he needed to be more open-minded about Olivia's predicament.

"He is in a difficult situation," Joseph said, knowing it may mean *he* would feel Richard Seymour's wrath.

Mr. Seymour nodded. "You are right, son. I'll apologize to the sheriff next time I see him. Now," he said, shifting in his chair, "where can we secure accommodation?"

Mrs. Baker raised her eyebrows. Joseph knew exactly what she was thinking – that Richard Seymour wouldn't be happy with any of the offerings available. "There is the men's boarding house, but they have little available, and may even be full. Or there's the saloon, which is not exactly ideal." Joseph scratched his head. "To be honest, neither is what you would be used to." He felt almost embarrassed to say it out loud, but knew his words to be true.

Mr. Seymour pierced him with a glare. "Are there no other alternatives?" His frustration was evident.

Mrs. Baker cleared her throat. "If you don't mind me saying so, Mr. Seymour, Grand Falls is a small, out-of-the-way town. We don't generally have people such as yourself stopping here."

"I take your point," he mumbled.

After some discussion, it was decided the bodyguards would stay at the saloon, and Mr. Seymour would stay with Joseph. His wasn't high class accommodation either, but at least it was a better option that the saloon, which could be downright disgusting.

They finished up their coffee, and two of the bodyguards stayed at the cottage to take up protection duties of Olivia, while the other two went to the saloon to secure rooms for them all.

Knowing Olivia was well protected now, Joseph was free to return to his home and resume his work. *Why was it then, he felt the ping of heartache at the thought of not seeing her every day?*

"Mr. Davis," Mrs. Baker said as he went to leave. "Please continue to have your meals here. We've both enjoyed your company. Haven't we, Olivia?"

Heat rose up Olivia's face, but the younger woman nodded. "We certainly have," she said, a smile on her face. Her smile quickly disappeared with the glare she received from her overly protective father.

Mrs. Baker turned to Olivia's father then. "You and your men are welcome as well."

Joseph's accommodations were not huge. Certainly nothing like Richard Seymour would be used to. His home was above his store, and was the same place he was raised.

Mr. Seymour glanced about. "I must thank you for allowing me to stay here with you," he said. "I understand it's an inconvenience." He continued to look around. "It's not huge, is it?"

Joseph swallowed. "No, Sir, I guess it's not when compared to where you live. But it's my childhood home. It accommodated three of us comfortably." He indicated for the other man to sit down on the well-worn couch, and Joseph placed the other man's overnight bag on the floor. "We don't put on airs here in Grand Falls. We live simply, but it's a good life."

"How is business? Do you make enough to support a family?" Joseph was surprised at the sudden change of topic, but understood where this was coming from. Mrs. Baker had said it was plain to see they were smitten with each other on more than one occasion. Mr. Seymour had only recently arrived, yet he seemed to have already noticed.

"I'm not overwhelmed with work, if that's what you mean. I live a comfortable life and have a steady stream of orders. If I had a family, which I don't, they would be well looked after."

The other man nodded. Despite the questions, Joseph was certain Olivia's father would not want her to marry someone of his standing. And frankly, he didn't blame him. Any parent would want the best for their child, especially when that child was used to far better.

"I imagine you are exhausted from your long trip. Let me show you the guest bedroom." He stood and the other man followed. Joseph indicated for him to enter the room that was once his own room. He'd since redecorated it, albeit very basic. It no longer looked like a child's room, but a welcoming room for a weary guest.

"I'm used to traveling, but not under such primitive conditions," he said, referring to the last stage of their journey on the stagecoach. Joseph imagined the five large men sardined into the coach and cringed. Each of the bodyguards were muscular men, and they alone would take up a lot of space, and he felt for this man who was not used to traveling in such a way. "I might have a nap, if you don't mind, that is."

"Not at all. I will go downstairs to my workshop to allow you some quiet time. I'll wake you for supper."

Mr. Seymour chuckled. "I won't nap that long," he said firmly. Joseph wasn't convinced.

Joseph pounded the leather. He was still smarting at not being able to spend as much time with Olivia.

The more he thought about it, though, the more he realized it could only be a good thing. They were getting far too friendly and too familiar with each other. *What would her father have said if he'd seen the way Joseph held her, or the way he'd caressed her cheek?*

Joseph had absolutely no doubt her father would be furious. Especially given Joseph was supposed to be her protector, and there he was, endearing himself to her instead. Only that's not what he was doing. He was comforting her. The fact it made him feel good too shouldn't come into it.

He'd never felt this way about a woman before, and it scared him to feel the things he felt for Olivia. Given her father would likely whisk her away at any given moment, he knew he would be a fool to continue to spend time with her. But to suddenly withdraw would not only hurt her feelings, it would be an pain he didn't want to endure.

The bell over his door tinkled, and more than ever, Joseph wished he had a glass panel in his workshop to see who was there. "Coming," he called.

It surprised him to see Richard Seymour standing in the middle of his store. "Did you sleep well? You look less tired."

"My tiredness came more from the worry about my little girl. Thank you again for looking after her." He reached out his hand and Joseph took it. It was clear this man was grateful to him, but he would be quick to take her back to Helena. Joseph was certain of it. "Do you have time to talk?"

Joseph indicated one of the chairs he had in the store for customers, then sat down opposite him. "What is the possibility these men are here in Grand Falls?"

"They're here. I saw them with my own eyes."

Richard eyes opened wide in astonishment. "And Olivia confirmed it was them?"

"She did. They didn't see her, but she identified them as the men who kidnapped her." He then relayed Olivia's story to her father about what lead to her being here in town. The color drained out of the other man's face, and Joseph regretted having told him, but knew it was something he needed to know.

"My poor baby girl." Joseph wanted to comfort him, but wasn't sure if he should. Richard Seymour seemed like the sort of man who wouldn't take sympathy well. "Right," he said, now standing. "We must move forward." His stomach rumbled, and heat rose in his face. "My apologies. It's been a while since I ate."

"Mrs. Baker will fix that," Joseph said, then chuckled. "Her food is excellent. She used to own and run the diner here in town, you know."

"No, I didn't know." He grinned, and Joseph understood Richard was looking forward to supper, just as he was.

It was supper for eight with all the bodyguards invited, and the table was full to the brim. "I apologize for the state of this meal," Mrs. Baker said, looking embarrassed. "I hadn't planned for guests."

Joseph stared at the platter sitting in the center of the table. "There is nothing wrong with this meal," he said firmly.

"I agree," Olivia's father said. "Roast chicken with vegetables. And it smells delicious."

"The vegetables are homegrown," Olivia added. "Mrs. Baker has a small patch out the back."

At her request, Joseph carved the chickens, then served. She had two large jugs of gravy — one for each end of the table. "We are truly grateful for the meal," Richard said. "I believe you are an excellent cook. It certainly smells that way." He smiled at her, and Joseph saw Mrs. Baker wilt under his compliment. It was strange because she'd endured years of compliments via the diner, but not from someone who came from high society.

"Wait until you taste it before deciding," she said, then laughed.

His plate was now full, and Richard took a mouthful. "This truly is delicious. Better than anything my cook back home has ever made."

Of course he'd have his own personal cook. The man owned several businesses in and around Helena. He was no doubt used to being waited on hand and foot. Joseph now realized that would be the case for Olivia as well. Despite that, she'd adapted well to small town living. Not that she'd had a lot of choice. This was where she'd landed, and to keep safe, it was where she had to stay.

For now, anyway. There was no doubt in Joseph's mind her father would take her home as soon as it was deemed safe to do so.

"Seriously," he said when Mrs. Baker frowned. "I wish I'd known you years ago. I would have employed you."

"You couldn't pay me enough to live in a big city," she said, almost under her breath. Everyone laughed.

Richard glanced up at her. "How long have you lived here, if you don't mind me asking?"

She stared into space momentarily, and Joseph knew from his own experience, memories were flooding her mind. "I was born here. And don't you dare ask how long ago that was." She said the latter firmly.

Laughter filled the room again. Joseph was enjoying the banter and laughter that filled the room. He'd missed that from when he'd lost his parents. Meals had always been a happy time in their home. When he began eating with Mrs. Baker, he felt remnants of the old days. Eating alone was not something he savored, but as a single man, he had little choice.

"What about you, Joseph?" He glanced across the table at Olivia's father. "Were you also born here?"

"Yes, Sir," he said firmly. "But not as long ago as Mrs. Baker." He continued to enjoy the laughter, but more than anything, he enjoyed watching Olivia's stress subside. She looked much more relaxed now, and that could only be a good thing.

"Cheeky," Mrs. Baker said in mirth. She smiled at him, and Joseph felt as though he was becoming like family to her. She certainly felt like part of his family now. Funny how he'd lived in this town all his life, but barely knew one of the best known characters in Grand Falls.

That was on him, and Joseph knew it. He kept to himself most of the time, either in his apartment above his store, or locked away in his workshop. He really needed to get out more. And he absolutely had to get a panel cut out of the workshop wall. It was claustrophobic in there at times. He was certain Patrick Harper, who did a lot of carpentry work around town, could do that for him. Right now was not the time, though. It as more important was to ensure Olivia was safe and got home unharmed. Now the bodyguards had arrived, that seemed very achievable.

The table was cleared and the desserts served. "You really are spoiling us, Mrs. Baker," one of the bodyguards said as he rubbed his belly. "I haven't eaten this well for…I can't recall when."

Apple and rhubarb pie was placed in the center of the table, along with bread pudding, custard pie and leftover chocolate cake from the night before. Last of all, a bowl of clotted cream was added.

"Oh my gosh!" Richard said. "I reaffirm what I said earlier. This is far better than anything my cook has ever served up."

"Olivia helped."

Richard Seymour stared at her in amazement. "*My Olivia?* Well, I'll be darned." He appeared truly shocked at the revelation. "She's never cooked a day in her life."

"All women should learn to cook," Mrs. Baker admonished. "Even the rich ones. You never know what will happen down the track to change their status." She stared at him until he shifted in his seat.

He turned to his daughter and his face softened. "I'm sorry, Olivia. We will rectify the situation when we get you back home. I'll arrange for a chef to come to the house and teach you. Your sister as well."

Olivia rolled her eyes. "I'm not interested in that. Mrs. Baker is teaching me to make practical food."

She reached out under from under the table and placed her hand in Joseph's. What he would do when she was gone, he didn't know. He knew he'd let himself get far too close to this wonderful but scared woman. He'd already spent far too much time with her and knew it had to stop.

"Thank you for a wonderful meal," Joseph said as he stood. "If you don't mind, I have things to attend to in my workshop."

"Of course you do," Mrs. Baker said. "I expect you back for breakfast," she said firmly.

He nodded, then headed toward the front door. "Come over when you are ready, Mr. Seymour." He left then, and didn't turn back. He already missed Olivia, despite her still being in town.

Chapter Six

Olivia was dreading going back home.

She liked it here in this small town – the people here were far more friendly than those in Helena. The place was full of hustle and bustle, with everyone in a hurry to get wherever it was they wanted to go. Grand Falls was the total opposite.

No one here was in a hurry, and although she'd not experienced much of the place, she had already fallen in love with it. When all this nonsense with kidnappers was over, she would breach the situation with her father – try to convince him to let her stay. She already knew what his answer would be.

A definite no.

So far, the kidnappers had kept themselves hidden away. *Surely they couldn't do that for much longer? Where were they staying? What were they eating?* She wondered if they'd have the audacity to stay in the saloon where the bodyguards were staying when they weren't protecting her.

They took turns with shifts – two men for each shift, and they stayed in Mrs. Baker's house for the duration. Her father, bless his heart, had arranged for a vast supply of food to be delivered to the cottage to make up for all the food they were eating.

"You really didn't need to do that, Richard," she admonished when it arrived. "I'm happy to help."

"You've done so much already," he answered. "I certainly wouldn't allow you to be out of pocket. I've also paid for a year's supply of wood to be chopped and delivered. It's the least I can do."

Olivia was impressed. She couldn't recall seeing her father do such a thing before, but she also didn't see a lot of him at home.

"Thank you," Mrs. Baker said, her cheeks now a bright pink. "I appreciate it." A knock at the door interrupted them. One of the bodyguards opened the door gingerly. After all, what sort of kidnappers would knock? They'd be more likely to break in during the night. Olivia knew it was true and was obviously what Joseph had thought since he slept close to the front door.

She heard her father sigh and glanced up from her chair in the sitting room. It was Cecil from the mercantile, delivering the order he had arranged. The box was huge, and he could barely carry it.

"Thank you, Mr. Delbert, that is very kind of you," Richard Seymour said. "Don't forget our arrangement."

Cecil Delbert nodded. He walked through the house and placed the box of groceries on the kitchen table. Something he'd no doubt done many times before.

He glanced curiously at Mrs. Baker, then turned his attention to Olivia. "Thank you, Mr. Delbert," Mrs. Baker said, then walked him out to the door. Normally her hostess would likely linger and engage in conversation with a visitor, even if he owned the mercantile. The current situation demanded she encourage him to leave the premises as quickly as possible.

Oliva was convinced her father was overreacting, especially with all these men he'd employed who were effectively personal guards. She winced at the thought. *What would the people in town think? Then again, had they even noticed?*

She could see Mr. Delbert wanted to ask what was going on, but was far too polite to do so. He must have noticed the number of people loitering in Mrs. Baker's cottage. They almost filled the place.

Mrs. Baker hurried back out to the kitchen and pulled everything out of the large box. "Honestly, Richard, this really is too much." She continued unpacking, and Olivia stepped in to help.

"It really isn't," her father said. "You went above and beyond the call of duty to look after my little girl – someone who is a complete stranger."

She smiled across at Olivia. "Not anymore, she's not. Besides, what sort of Christian would I be if I ignored someone who needed help?" She reached up to place some groceries in the overhead cupboards. It didn't make sense to Olivia, since Mrs. Baker was quite small in stature.

"Let me help," Richard said, stepping closer.

"Why do you have them up so high?" Olivia wanted to know.

"My late husband was far taller than me; he always helped by passing them down." *Her husband who had passed on many years ago? Yet she continued to put everything in cupboards she couldn't reach?* It made no sense to Olivia. "I can't bring myself to move things around." She turned her back on Olivia and she realized she'd upset the dear lady.

"What if I help with moving things about?"

"Olivia," her father said sternly. "It's not your business."

"It's all right," Mrs. Baker said. "I should have done it years ago. If you help me clear out those lower cupboards, we can store the groceries there. I've been meaning to have a pantry added for as long as I can remember. When Henry died, I didn't bother.

"Who would you get to do that?" Richard asked.

Mrs. Baker waved his words away. "We have a skilled carpenter in Grand Falls, Patrick Harper, but I'm far too old to worry about such things now." She continued to reorganize her groceries with Olivia's help.

Olivia's father left the room, and she heard some low murmuring, then the front door opening, then closing. He was obviously up to something, and Olivia was sure she knew what it was.

"There. All done. Now I have to remember where everything is," Mrs. Baker said, before she turned and refilled the kettle to prepare coffee for everyone.

Olivia wondered what Joseph was doing. Despite have slept there last night, her father hadn't mentioned him at all. She desperately wanted to visit him, but knew it wasn't safe for her. Well, according to her father, anyway. There had been no sign of the kidnappers for around a week, so that likely meant they had given up and left the area.

According to her bodyguards, they were lying low, waiting for the perfect opportunity. According to Olivia's reasoning, they'd be fools to hang around when she had so much protection. She wanted to go outside in the fresh air. She wanted to taste freedom again, but more than anything else, she wanted to see Joseph.

She missed him and wasn't afraid to say it.

"Here's your tea, Olivia." Mrs. Baker's voice brought her back to reality, which was probably just as well. Dreaming of a life with Joseph was nothing short of foolish. As soon as it was deemed safe, she would travel back home with her father and the four men secured to protect her. She dreaded it. Going back to Helena after the peacefulness of Grand Falls felt like a step down.

She didn't miss the dances, or the parties, or even the gentlemen callers. Her father had been grooming her for marriage since she turned eighteen, but that was not the life Olivia wanted for herself. But she could see herself living here. With Joseph.

The trouble was, her father would never agree. He believed, and had told her frequently, she had to marry someone of her own social standing. Money meant nothing to Olivia. Love meant everything.

Over the short time she'd known him, Olivia had grown to love Joseph. He had given up everything for her – his business had surely suffered, and she was certain the pallet wouldn't have been the most comfortable place to sleep, and yet he'd endured it night after night almost since the day she'd arrived. *And wasn't it Joseph who had saved her from herself? If he hadn't intervened, where would she be now?*

More than likely, those horrible men who'd plucked her off the streets of Helena would have grabbed her right here in Grand Falls. A place that had never seen such shenanigans before. At least according to Mrs. Baker, and she should know.

"What are you thinking about?" Her father's voice whispering in her ear brought Olivia's daydreaming to an end. "You seem to do a lot of woolgathering lately. I don't recall seeing you do that back home."

She wanted to turn and remind him he rarely saw her back home. This was the longest time she'd seen Richard Seymour for many years. When her mother died, he threw himself into his work, and a governess cared for the children. Once her brothers were old enough to help with the business, they began their training to take over when the time came. His daughters were left to their own devices because they weren't important to Father's business. Their future was nothing more than being married off to a man whose family was equally prosperous.

Tears formed in Olivia's eyes and she tried to fight them back. After all, she'd been taught all her life not to cry. Hot tears rolled down her face unbidden, and no matter what she did, Olivia could not hold them back.

There was a knock at the door, and she heard scrambling as the bodyguards did their job and checked it out. She felt like she was in a haze – everything was in the background, nothing seemed real. Voices murmured, and she felt herself being pulled gently out of her chair. "Olivia." Joseph's sweet voice filled her head, but he wasn't here.

Then she found herself in his arms. Joseph pulled her close and wrapped his arms around her. His hands making circles on her back had her relaxing a little. She felt his warm lips on her forehead, and she settled into him, her head on his chest. She felt comfortable with him, and safe. Despite the paid protection her father had brought with him, Joseph was the one who made her feel safe.

"Shock has finally set in," Richard Seymour said.

Joseph kissed her forehead again before he spoke. "She was in shock when she arrived. This is something else, I'm certain."

"If you think you know my daughter better than I do…"

Mrs. Baker interrupted him. "Why don't you two sit in the garden? It's nice out there today."

Olivia didn't wait to hear what her father had to say about that, and neither did Joseph. He guided her outside and onto the crude wooden bench that Henry Baker had no doubt made many years ago.

"I don't want to leave here," she said once they were settled. "I like it here."

Joseph studied her, and his face softened. "I doubt your father would agree." She stared up into his eyes. He was a kind man, one she would like to know far better.

"I am a grown woman, an adult," she said firmly. "He can't control me, even if he would like to." She leaned into Joseph then, knowing full well what she said, and what actually happened were two totally different things.

Chapter Seven

Joseph was happy to sit out in the garden with Olivia for as long as it took. He had never taken much notice of the area before, but realized this was a place where someone could climb the fence and have clear access to the house.

He wondered why the bodyguards hadn't scrutinize it. Wasn't that part of their job? He shook his head. To be honest, he didn't know the garden existed until recently, so he could understand their lack of knowledge. He'd spent far more time at Mrs. Baker's house in the past week or so than the bodyguards had.

It begged the question whether or not the kidnappers had hidden out in this garden waiting for a chance to grab Olivia. Was that the reason they hadn't been seen? They could easily hide underneath some of the larger plants.

He silently thanked the Lord he had escorted the ladies out here when they came to get vegetables for their cooking endeavors. If he hadn't…he didn't want to even think about it.

"Feeling better?" he whispered. He didn't want to alert Olivia to the danger that might be facing them. She nodded, and he stood, glancing about as he did, not willing to take a chance on Olivia's life. He gently pushed her ahead of him and through the back door. Once he had her settled in the sitting room, he headed straight to the bodyguards. They both scuttled outside, and Joseph followed them.

He heard Richard Seymour follow behind him. "What's going on?" He sounded more confused than anything. Joseph explained, setting his mind to rest.

Joseph suddenly halted. The women were unprotected. *What if the kidnappers were watching them and realized they'd left the house unguarded?* His heart thudded in his chest. He admonished himself for his stupidity and rushed back inside. "I hope you boys are not raiding my garden," Mrs. Baker said, sounding a little annoyed, while at the same time smirking.

"I hadn't thought about the dangers out there," he said quietly, sounding defeated even to himself.

"Piffle," Mrs. Baker said, waving a hand in the air. "They wouldn't do anything in broad daylight, surely."

Until this moment, Olivia had sat quietly, listening to the conversation but not saying a word. "It was the middle of the day when they snatched me in Helena," she hissed. "It was my fault – they said Father had sent them to collect me. I should have realized. My father had no interest in me and wouldn't even know where I was or what I was doing." She glanced down at her lap. "I was a fool." Tears ran down her cheeks again, and Joseph went to her.

"Did you ask to be kidnapped, to be treated so shabbily?" She shook her head, the tears still falling. He wiped them away with his fingers. "Then how can it be your fault?" He pulled her out of the chair and comforted her. Despite all the protection she now had, it was clear to Joseph that Olivia did not feel safe. At least not from her feelings of guilt.

Mrs. Baker watched their every move; a slight smile touched her lips. He was certain she approved, although she didn't say as much.

"I should get lunch sorted," she said, then hurried into the kitchen. "You're eating with us, Mr. Davis," she called over her shoulder, then busied herself, not giving him a chance to refuse. Not that he wanted to – Joseph wanted to spend as much time as possible with Olivia. No doubt Richard Seymour would whisk her away soon. He'd already said as much.

The question was, would Olivia go willingly, or would her father force her to leave when she didn't want to?

The man in question entered the room. "Olivia," he bellowed, "pull yourself together."

Joseph felt her stiffen. He glanced up and glared at Richard Seymour. "She has every right to be distressed. I'm sure if you were in the same situation, you would feel that way too."

He could see the other man fighting with himself. Joseph didn't care if he was on the wrong end of his wrath, provided he left Olivia alone.

"Don't you have a business to run?" her father asked gruffly.

Joseph shifted slightly. The air was tense, and he could see Olivia's father was readying himself for an argument, but Joseph was not the arguing type. He lived a peaceful life and rarely had a cross word with anyone. He wasn't about to start now.

"Your daughter is my priority," he said, ensuring there was no tension in his voice. He pulled her closer and wrapped his arms around her once more. He glanced down, and she was looking up at him. A brief smile flashed before him, but it was gone as quickly as it had arrived. He was tempted to kiss her, but Joseph was certain Richard would have something to say about that, too.

He didn't blame Richard, he was being a protective father. *The question was, where was he when she really needed him?* From what Olivia had said, he had never been around, and had little time for her. *But now he wanted to fix that? Or was it that he needed everyone to see he was a good father to her?*

87

Either way, Joseph was not impressed with the other man's pretense. He might believe he was a good father, and appearances would say that was correct. Only Joseph knew better. Richard's business and money were far more important to him than his daughters. He hadn't even noticed Olivia was missing for some days. The sheriff told him it wasn't until the governess reported her missing many days later that a missing person alert was posted. It was the entire reason Sheriff Saxon didn't know who she was.

"Lunch is ready," Mrs. Baker announced. "Sit yourselves down." She glanced from Richard to Joseph. It was clear she realized something was wrong, but she'd missed all the fireworks.

It was then Joseph noticed the bodyguards were back in the room. He'd been far too busy with Olivia, and also her obnoxious father, to even notice.

Olivia pulled out of Joseph's arms and getting up on her tip-toes, place a brief kiss on his lips. His whole body sang. He heard the gasp from her father and wondered if Olivia had kissed him with the sole purpose of angering her father.

He glanced down at her, and a smile split her face. She reached out and took both his hands, squeezing them tight, then dropping them right before heading into the kitchen.

One thing he knew for certain, the conversation in his apartment this evening would not be pleasant. He would prepare himself for an earbashing from Richard Seymour tonight.

"The food was delicious, as always, Edna." Richard Seymour was good at giving out compliments to Mrs. Baker, but terrible at treating his daughter like an adult.

"It certainly was," Joseph added. He sat next to Olivia at the table. She always placed herself there, but he wasn't complaining. He wiped his lips with a linen napkin, then rose.

"You're not going already?" Mrs. Baker's protest left him wondering if she didn't like the prospect of being here with all these men. Men who, only days ago, were complete strangers. He was certain they were trustworthy – they wouldn't be employed by Richard Seymour otherwise – but that didn't mean she felt comfortable with them. He picked up his soiled dishes and headed toward the kitchen, knowing his hostess would likely follow him.

He placed his dishes in the bowl of soapy water. "Olivia's father doesn't like me. It's better if I make myself scarce."

Her lips formed into a tight line. "Olivia needs you. Richard is just looking out for his daughter."

"Smothering her more like it. I must go anyway. I have something to organize."

"Like what?" Mrs. Baker pierced him with her eyes – eyes that never missed a thing. He got the impression she didn't believe a word he said.

Joseph squirmed under her scrutiny. "I need to find Patrick Harper. I've wanted a window panel in my workshop for years. Now is as good a time as any to get it done." The older woman studied him. "I can't see anything that goes on outside my workshop," he said. "I can't see customers when they arrive, and they can't see me. If that work was already done, I might spot the kidnappers, since I know what they look like."

Mrs. Baker reached out and took both his hands. "It a good idea, but please be careful. Olivia would be devastated if anything happened to you." She leaned in and hugged him then, and Joseph was taken aback. She had never been this familiar with him before. She barely knew him until Olivia had arrived in town. He now knew that was his loss. He'd kept himself to himself, and that wasn't necessarily a good thing.

After all this was over, Joseph needed to consider widening his web of friends. He liked Mrs. Baker, and it made him wonder how many other people in Grand Falls he would like. Or who would like him.

He knew most people who lived and around the area, but only because they bought their boots from him. His boots were renowned for their quality, so folks came from miles around to buy them.

"Thank you for caring," he said, and the older woman studied him.

"Of course I care," she said. "Even before these recent events, I cared. I knew you as a child, but you probably don't remember – you were quite young."

He stared at her. Joseph didn't remember her from his childhood, not at all. She reached for his hands again and squeezed them. "When all this is over, I do hope we can keep in touch."

"Of course," he said, then turned and left before his emotions overcame him. It had been years since anyone told Joseph they cared. It was also far too long since he'd taken an interest in anyone beyond the fleeting relationship he had with his customers.

His first stop was at the mercantile. If anyone knew where he could find Patrick Harper, it would be Cecil Delbert. He knew most everyone, and often their movements. Luckily for Joseph, the mercantile owner knew exactly where he could find the town carpenter.

It wasn't long before he'd caught up with Patrick and explained his requirements. Patrick was just finishing up for the day, and promised to call by Joseph's store in the next half hour.

"I can't believe what an enormous difference this makes," Joseph said as Patrick began packing up his tools. "It's far brighter than I expected."

"The glass still needs to be installed of course, but it shouldn't be too long." Joseph knew he could rely on Patrick. Since he'd arrived in Grand Falls, he'd earned the respect of everyone who knew him. "I'll do the other window when the glass arrives."

Patrick was still packing up when Richard Seymour arrived. The good thing was he saw Olivia's father before he'd even entered the store. He felt himself stiffen. No doubt he'd come to talk about that kiss. The one that was totally unexpected. He put his fingers to his lips at the memory, and as much as he'd enjoyed Olivia's lips on his, he wished she hadn't because he couldn't shake it from his mind.

He knew he was only delaying the inevitable, but introduced Patrick to Richard Seymour. "Good to meet you," Richard said, shaking the other man's hand. "I was going to contact you – I have a job for you, and I need it done sooner than later." Patrick stared at him. Joseph had introduced him as a visitor to town, so it was apparent he didn't live here. "I would like you to build a generous sized pantry for Edna Baker. I've checked, and there's plenty of space." Patrick continued to study him, which didn't sit well with Richard. "I'll pay you triple your normal fee to do this in the next day or so."

"What does Mrs. Baker think about your plan?" Patrick appeared wary, and Joseph didn't blame him one bit.

"She doesn't know," Richard admitted. "I want it to be a surprise. A gift from me."

Patrick ran a hand through his hair. "I have no problem building a pantry for her, but not without her permission."

"See here, young man," Richard said gruffly. "Do you know who I am?"

The carpenter studied him again. "No idea, but it makes no difference. I will not change Mrs. Baker's home without her approval. It's as simple as that." He snapped his toolbox closed, then stood. "I'm happy to go there with you now and check with her."

Richard did not look happy yet again, but he followed Patrick out the door. Joseph needed fresh air and went outside. He was pleased he finally had the window he'd promised himself years ago, and believed it would make a tremendous difference to him.

Chapter Eight

Olivia sat back in the comfortable chair in the sitting room. Her father was agitated, pacing back and forth despite the cramped room. It was partly because of that kiss she'd placed on Joseph's lips, she was certain. She smiled smugly. It was pastime her father understood she was a grown woman, and as such she got to make her own decisions, and that included who she married.

Her mind wandered. She couldn't stop thinking about the kiss, brief as it was.

Moments before she'd kissed him, Olivia's heart thudded in anticipation. She'd only done it to annoy her father, to show him she was an adult, and he had no right to boss her around as if she was one of his employees.

The moment their lips met, she wanted to linger longer. Shivers traveled down her spine, and she felt good all over. Warmth had flooded her. Olivia had liked Joseph more and more every time she saw him, and when their fingers met, heat flooded her. Finally, she'd come to the conclusion she loved him.

The problem was, Olivia had never loved anyone before, except for her family, that was. *How could she know what love was? Perhaps she'd come to admire Joseph for rendering assistance when it was needed, despite the potential danger it put him in?*

When they were alone, she might have to talk to Mrs. Baker about it. She sighed. She risked sounding like a foolish teenager, and that was the last thing she wanted.

Olivia put her fingers to her lips. She could still taste him; it almost felt like his lips were still on hers.

"Olivia!" her father bellowed. "Are you even listening to me?" Well, no. She truly wasn't. It was far more fun daydreaming about Joseph Davis. She stared at her father, then stood.

"If you can't treat me with respect, I have no time for you, Father." She glanced over his shoulder to look at the two bodyguards who appeared shocked. Never before had she stood up to her father. No one dared challenge Richard Seymour. Not once had she seen it happen.

Well, now she'd done it, and she would do it again if necessary. At twenty-four, she was no longer a child, and she refused to be treated as one.

"Olivia Seymour, you come back here." Despite her father's bellowing, she ignored him and went out into the garden, her bodyguards scampering behind her. She sat on the same bench she'd shared with Joseph not all that long ago and wished he was here now. What she wanted now was to clarify her feelings. She learned little about real life at the Swiss finishing school, and that's what a young woman really needed.

She glanced up as Mrs. Baker came into the garden. "Are you all right, my dear?" She sat down beside Olivia. She'd probably done it thousands of times with her husband. She put an arm around Olivia and pulled her close. "You realize your father is worried about you, I'm certain. So perhaps think about how *he* is feeling right now."

She was right, of course, but Olivia also had feelings. "What's it like to love someone?" She glanced down into her lap, not being brave enough to look Mrs. Baker in the eye. *Would her hostess think her a fool?*

When she glanced up again, the other woman's face had softened. "Love is…a lot of things," she said, appearing whimsical. "It's wanting to be with the other person when they aren't with you, feeling a tingle in your fingers when you touch, being filled with warmth when they hold you." She waved a hand in the air. "Love is so much more. It would take days, perhaps even months, to explain it."

Olivia was floored. She did not know how to respond to Mrs. Baker's explanation. Everything she'd said described how she felt exactly. *Did that mean she was in love with Joseph?* She wasn't sure how she felt about that. Particularly since she would leave soon. At least, according to her father.

Hot tears rolled down her cheeks, and Olivia swiped at them. She'd shed far more tears here in Grand Falls than she'd ever shed at home. Perhaps it was because she felt more relaxed here, despite her situation. She loved this little town, and she never wanted to leave. But what sort of a way to earn an income. The only true skill she had was advising women on fashion — what clothes and colors suited them. If only a town like this supported such a business.

"It's Joseph, isn't it?" Mrs. Baker whispered, despite them being alone. The bodyguards were at the other end of the garden out of earshot, but close enough to ensure Olivia was safe.

Olivia turned to face the older woman. "It is," she whispered. "And I don't want to lose him."

Mrs. Baker tapped a finger on her chin. "That could be a problem, especially if your father has anything to do with it." Olivia felt herself angering. Richard Seymour might be her father, but that didn't mean he got to rule her life.

Something suddenly alerted Olivia to her father's presence, and she felt her anger deepening. *She wasn't a child anymore!* She suddenly stood, lifted her skirts, ran past her father, and into the house. The two bodyguards ran after her, but she'd taken them unawares and they weren't quick enough. Olivia slammed the front door behind her and ran toward Joseph's store.

Olivia heard pounding feet behind her, and pushed herself up against the wall. Her heart pounded – whether that was from running or sheer terror, she wasn't sure. What she knew was she felt as though she was suffocating. Her father became worse every time she saw him, and even at Mrs. Baker's house, she felt as though he was trying to push her down to the level of her employees and servants, and force her to do what *he* wanted. Richard Seymour had got his own way for as long as she could remember.

When her mother was alive, she'd taken the brunt of his bullying behavior. Why she had put up with it, Olivia never understood. *It was a woman's lot,* her mother would say, but Olivia knew better. It was a woman's right to be treated with respect, not to be downtrodden by her husband.

Joseph wasn't like that. Funny that she thought of him in her hour of need.

The running sound got closer, and she prayed it was her bodyguards. She could only imagine the wrath they would receive from her father. He would be furious that she escaped them, not to mention she'd raced past him with little effort.

Surely by now the danger had passed?

She sensed someone nearby before she heard them. When she turned, Olivia's heart felt like it would leave her chest. *It was them.* The two putrid criminals who had kidnapped her. Why would they continue to pursue her after all this time? And where had they been hiding out? It was some weeks since she'd arrived in Grand Falls, which meant they were persistent, if nothing else.

Olivia finally came to her senses and ran. The tall one reached out and grabbed at her, but she was too fast, and he only managed to tear at her shirt. She heard herself screaming as she ran for her life, but no one was around. Not even the bodyguards. To her detriment, she'd achieved what she set out to do – lose them.

No one knew where she was, or that she was in eminent danger.

It had become a pleasure to stand in the workshop making boots.

Joseph had decided years ago to have a window panel created in his workshop. He couldn't believe the amount of additional light he'd gained. The bonus was he no longer felt suffocated in the small room where he created beautiful and functional boots for customers who came from near and far.

He smiled as he looked out over the road and toward the diner. There were a few people about, but not many. Mrs. Thompson entered the diner, and Mrs. White followed soon after. He noticed more ladies from the church auxiliary enter the diner as well. *How long had they been meeting at the diner? he wondered. How much of life in Grand Falls had Joseph missed?* It saddened him to think he'd closed himself off to the rest of the town, but he felt joyful he'd finally taken the plunge. It didn't take Patrick long to make the adjustments – at least not as long as Joseph had expected. Once the glass panel arrived, it would look even better.

Seeing those selfless women entering the diner made him decide a coffee would be nice. It was a chilly day, and the store was cool despite the roaring fire he always kept alight. He rubbed his hands together, trying to warm them, to no avail.

He went to the fire and warmed his hands. It was difficult to work when his hands were almost frozen. As he squatted in front of the fire, he thanked the Lord for the blessings he had. In his father's day, life was tough. Arthur Davis worked long hours and saw little of his family. Joseph vowed never to make the same mistakes his father had made .

He picked up his leather hammer, ready to pound the leather in front of him. That's when he heard it. Uncertain what he'd heard, Joseph hesitated. There it was again. The sound was muffled and he couldn't make out what he was hearing, so went outside. As he stepped outside, the muffled sound became a scream. A long and heartbreaking scream.

When he glanced toward the sound, his heart shattered. Olivia ran toward him, two scruffy men in pursuit and they certainly weren't her protectors. Oh, they were there and running toward her, but were not close enough to help her, as much as they tried. Joseph was far closer and rushed to her aid.

His sensibilities kicked in as well as his level of fury, which was above anything he'd ever experienced before. *How dare these men endeavor to steal Olivia from those who loved her?* Joseph had grown to love her over the short time they'd known each other; only weeks, but weeks packed with memories and plenty of emotion.

He had never moved so fast, and never felt so enraged his entire life. The abductors were so engrossed in their efforts, they hadn't even noticed him, which was fine by Joseph. He had the element of surprise with the first man and grabbed him by the arms and tossed him aside. The second was not so easy – he was now fully aware of the danger and pulled a gun. Joseph froze momentarily, then, coming to his senses, shoved Olivia behind him.

She screamed, but he was determined to ignore her pleading sounds.

Suddenly, the sound of gun shot filled the air.

Chapter Nine

Olivia's heart thudded. Her ears were ringing from the blast of the gun, and she was in a daze. It took long moments before she had her wits about her again.

Joseph! He'd been shot!

Yet he stood in front of her. He glanced over his shoulder at her as though nothing untoward had occurred. "Are you all right?" he asked urgently. She nodded, and he promptly turned her to face the other way.

"You're not shot?" Her voice sounded as breathless as she felt. It was as though the air had been punched out of her and it left nothing inside her. The kidnapper Joseph had tossed aside like a sack of flour was beginning to come around. One bodyguard was at his side before he had a chance to stand, let alone escape.

Joseph scowled at the two bodyguards. "You two were supposed to be protecting her." His words were gruff, and she glanced down to see his hands fisted. She'd never seen him so angry.

"She...got away," one of her protectors said, scowling and sounding defeated. Olivia understood she'd done the wrong thing, but so had they. She'd tried to have a private conversation and was not given that dignity. It had angered her to the point she couldn't think straight.

But it was over now. She was again free to roam the streets, go shopping if she wished, and eat at the diner – all without protection. More significantly, she could take a stroll with Joseph around Grand Falls, totally alone.

She let out a long sigh of relief.

"How are you doing?" Joseph asked quietly, standing close to her.

Olivia glanced up at him. "Thanks to you, I'm fine. Things could have turned out far worse." Somewhere in the distance she heard her father's voice. It sounded as though he was in an echo chamber and was miles away. The last thing she remembered was being held in Joseph's arms as she slowly slid to the ground.

"It's the shock," Doc Spencer said as he checked her over. It felt like déjà vu to Olivia. This was where her journey in Grand Falls had begun. At least that she could recall. It was Joseph who had saved her then as well.

Back then, she didn't know him. Not at all. But now she did, and she was far richer for his friendship.

She glanced across the doctor's room. Sheriff Earl Saxon stood guarding the man who'd been shot – one of her kidnappers. Her heart pounded at the thought and she tried to sit up. Joseph nuzzled her back down. "He can't hurt you," he said. "This one is in cuffs, the other one is in jail."

In her peripheral vision, Olivia saw her father stand. "I'm sorry, Father," she said softly.

"No, I'm sorry. Joseph has told me in no uncertain terms I shouldn't have been so heavy-handed. He's right." Richard Seymour looked at the floor. Olivia had never seen him so defeated. Not once in her life had she heard him apologize for anything, and the fact he had done so stunned her.

"If you feel up to it, you are free to leave," Doc Spencer said. "You've experienced a massive shock." He turned to Joseph and her father then. "Any sign she is not improving, dizziness, or any confusion, bring her back. Rest is the best medicine."

Joseph took her hand and helped Olivia to sit up. "Slowly. You don't want to get dizzy before you even get to leave." He helped her down from the surgery bed, and it was then she noticed Mrs. Baker sitting to the side.

"I was so scared," she said, tears shimmering in her eyes. The older woman went to her and hugged Olivia tight. It was the closest she'd ever seen to

Mrs. Baker becoming emotional. "I'm glad you're okay now." She pulled Olivia close again and held her tight. It was all Olivia could do not to cry. When she glanced across at Joseph, it was clear he'd been affected by the entire scenario. Even worse, she'd put his life in danger.

If one of the bodyguards hadn't shot the kidnapper, her abductor would have shot, and likely killed Joseph. The thought made her light-headed again, but she had no intention of telling anyone.

Joseph stepped forward and put an arm around her. *Had he guessed?* Perhaps her expression had given her away. She would likely never know.

"Do you feel up to going home?" Joseph's voice was slightly above a whisper, and only Olivia would have heard it. *Did he mean home to Helena, or was he referring to Mrs. Baker's house?* She was still dazed, Olivia was certain of it. Instead of showing her confusion, she nodded, hoping her confusion would soon subside.

Grand Falls felt like home now, and Helena seemed like a faraway memory.

"I don't know how to thank you." Richard Seymour sat in Joseph's apartment. "You saved Olivia's life."

There was far more emotion in his voice than Joseph had ever heard from him before. He leaned forward on the couch and gazed at the man who was around the same age his own father would have been now. "I won't say it was nothing. The experience was terrifying, but did you honestly think I would allow your daughter to be kidnapped yet again?" He shook his head in disbelief. "It was never going to happen, even if it meant they killed me in the process." He swallowed down the emotion he was feeling now. He really could have been slaughtered if Olivia's bodyguard hadn't shot first.

The color drained from Richard's face. "What can I do to make things right? I mean, there must be something you want. Something that was out of reach before. Money is no object."

Joseph didn't have to think about it. "Your daughter's hand in marriage. If she'll have me," he added.

Richard Seymour didn't seem surprised. "Does she know about this?"

"I haven't asked her, if that's what you mean. I love her more than life itself…"

"And you've proved it," Richard said quickly. "But despite that, I can't give you my blessing. Olivia has been brought up to expect more than…" He waved a hand around Joseph's apartment. "this. No offence, but my daughter deserves better."

Joseph stood then, filled with anger, but he fought his emotions. "Thankfully, it's not your choice," he said firmly. "Olivia is an adult, and can decide for herself."

"Tell me what you want – anything. As I said before, money is no object."

Joseph glared. "You can't buy me," he said furiously, then stormed out of the room and went to bed, hoping he would get some sleep, but knowing he probably wouldn't – not only because of the events of the day, but the rage he felt toward Olivia's father.

As much as Richard Seymour was the richest man in Helena if not Montana, all he could give Joseph, and all he wanted, was the man's sincere blessings.

Joseph reveled in being able to walk hand-in-hand with Olivia without worrying about kidnappers or bodyguards. The fact she was now safe was like gold to him.

"Father is returning to Helena in a day or two. We don't always see eye to eye, but getting to know him better has been…" She took a deep breath. "an experience." She smiled then, and Joseph understood what Olivia meant. Her father wasn't the easiest person to get on with. He was far too used to getting his own way. Even Mrs. Baker saw through him and cut him to the core when necessary. "He's asked me to go with him."

Joseph smiled then. Depending on her answer, Richard knew that more than likely, Olivia would not be returning home. "There's something I need to talk to you about." His words were soft, and if he was honest with himself, Joseph was unsure how to breach the subject. "Perhaps we could sit down for a bit," he said, guiding her toward the gazebo that was in the park.

Olivia stared at him curiously, but said nothing.

"Do you want to go back to Helena?" he asked quietly as he continued to hold her hand.

She stared at him, her eyes wide open in astonishment. "Not at all, but father is insisting."

She appeared quite sad then, and it broke his heart. Joseph knew it was now or never, and dropped to one knee. "Olivia Seymour," he said, not letting her hand go, "I know we've not known each other for a terribly long time, but over that time, I've grown to really like you." He licked his lips then. "To be honest, I've come to adore, and even love you." He stared directly into her eyes. Will you marry me?"

Olivia stared at him in amazement. "Marry you? Of course I will! But what will Father say?"

Joseph breathed a massive sigh of relief. "Your father refused to give his blessings." He refused to lie to her, and watched as she scowled.

"Of course he did," she said, sounding very annoyed. "Well, that's his problem, not ours."

He stood then and pulled Olivia to her feet. He pulled her close and hugged her, then kissed her right on the lips, and didn't care who was watching.

"We're supposed to be leaving in the next couple of days, when the stagecoach comes through next."

Joseph scrunched up his face. "You don't want to do that. Can you even imagine how tight it would be with six of you in one coach, and five of the six being big men?" He shook his head. "No, that won't do at all." He grinned at her then. "My idea is far better."

Pulling her closer, Joseph felt Olivia relax against him. "You're right, of course," she said firmly. "Father will just have to complain if he doesn't like it, but it won't get him anywhere." Her arms slipped around Joseph's waist and he couldn't believe how content he felt at that moment. He felt more joy now than he could ever remember feeling, and knew it was all because of Olivia.

Not that he would ever wish for her to endure what she'd been through, but if she wasn't kidnapped, she wouldn't have landed in Grand Falls. "Has anyone discovered how you arrived in Grand Falls?" Joseph asked, wary of even breaching the subject. The last thing he wanted was to upset her.

"The best Father could find was some good Samaritan bought a ticket for me and took me on the train, pretending I was with him." She glanced down at the ground, and her next words were almost a whisper. "I don't remember any of it. Anything could have happened." She blinked several times and Joseph knew she was fighting tears. He pulled her even closer and wrapped her in his love. Something he intended to do for the rest of her life.

Despite Richard's protests, the wedding was small. He admonished Joseph for going against his wishes, but finally accepted his youngest daughter was also a grown woman who had a mind of her own. He didn't like the fact his girls were adults and made their own decisions, but conceded there was little he could do about it.

The small church in Grand Falls was filled with locals for the impromptu wedding less than a week later. Olivia had stayed on at Mrs. Baker's cottage until the big day, giving her family time to arrive. Still living with Joseph, her father ensured she didn't see the groom until the big day.

Despite his request for a custom-made wedding gown from the finest boutique in Helena, Olivia wore a gown made by Grand Falls' very own tailor.

Joseph straightened his tie for the last time and glanced down the aisle. His heart fluttered at the vision of his soon-to-be wife standing next to her father. Despite his initial disapproval of their marriage, he stood proudly next to his daughter, his love for her written all over his face. Even if she'd worn an over-the-counter gown from Delbert's Mercantile, he knew she would be a sight to behold.

The organ began to play, and his heart pounded. This was the day he'd waited all his life for. Joseph only wished his parents were here to meet his wonderful wife. The moment they arrived at the front of the church, Richard handed his daughter over and joined their hands. *Was that a tear he saw on Richard Seymour's face?*

He smiled at Olivia, and they turned to face the preacher. Most of the service was lost on him, as Joseph spent far too much time woolgathering about their future.

"Joseph," Preacher Angus Devon said loudly. "You need to answer the question." He grinned at Joseph, who now felt flustered.

"I…I do. Of course I do!" he answered.

"Now place the ring on your wife's finger." He did as instructed, his heart pounding the entire time. "You may now kiss the bride."

Joseph didn't wait to be told again. He'd kissed Olivia twice since they'd met, and she instigated one of those kisses, and was so brief as to be almost a dream.

As they turned to leave the church, he noticed Mrs. Baker sitting in the front row next to Richard Seymour and his family. She smiled at him and nodded. The old dear looked proud as punch. Joseph knew almost from the start she had tried to match Olivia and himself, but he'd resisted her matchmaking.

Now he couldn't imagine why.

Instead of walking down the aisle with his wife, he strolled over to Mrs. Baker, his surrogate grandmother in many ways, and gently pulled the elderly woman to her feet. He pulled her into a bear hug. "Thank you," he whispered, holding her longer than necessary. Finally guiding her back to her seat, he turned to Richard Seymour. "I know you don't approve, but thank you. One day, you may come to care for me."

Joseph began to turn around, but Richard stopped him and took his hand, shaking it. "I didn't want to lose my daughter, but I now realize what I've actually done is gain a son. Welcome to the family," he said, and this time there was no doubt about the tears. Richard pulled Joseph into him, and the two men stood hugging each other for long moments. "Your wife is waiting for you," Richard finally said, and they parted.

Still feeling stunned at the other man's unexpected words, Joseph walked his new wife down the aisle, excited for their future together.

Epilogue

Three years later...

"Come to grandpapa," Richard Seymour coo'ed, opening his arms to two-year-old Arthur.

Olivia wandered into the sitting room of the large home her father had bought them as a wedding gift. At first, she scoffed at the gift, and so did Joseph. But a new home built by local carpenters Patrick Harper and Sawdust Harry, that was located on the edge of town, was not a gift to be shunned.

"Really, Father, you're spoiling him," Olivia said as she waddled into the room. As she was heavily pregnant, Richard Seymour had come to town to help. Not that it was necessary – they had friends all over town these days. Joseph had changed his reticent ways, and Olivia enjoyed the socialization when time allowed. "What will happen when you go back home?" She scowled, knowing that would be sooner than later if he got his way.

He studied her until Olivia squirmed under his gaze. "Father? What's going on? I know when you're withholding something." She squinted and studied him, just as he'd done to her.

The front door opened and Joseph stepped inside. "Papa!" Young Arthur greeted his father with joy, as he did every day.

The baby kicked and Olivia put a hand to her stomach. "Is everything all right?" Joseph asked, coming to stand beside his wife. He squatted down to her level and rubbed a gentle hand across her belly. She groaned then stood, her back ache far worse today.

Joseph rubbed her lower back, taking her mind off everything else. Until she recalled the conversation moments before he arrived. "Father?" He glanced up as though he hoped she'd forgotten.

"I wasn't going to say anything. Not yet anyway." Joseph continued to rub her back, and it felt good, but wasn't helping. "I've retired." After that bombshell, he clammed up and didn't say another word. Olivia groaned again. If she hadn't been in pain, she would surely have laughed. *Her father retire?* It had to be a joke. "I'm thinking about living right here in Grand Falls. None of my other children have made me a grandpapa, and this way, I'll be close should you need me."

"And what of the others?" Olivia said, not too unhappy about the situation. Her relationship with her father had improved tremendously since the wedding, and he'd visited several times. He kept in touch with Mrs Baker too, and despite them becoming great friends, he was still trying to convince her to let him install a pantry for her. The thought made Olivia smile.

The move to Grand Falls would do her father a lot of good, but she worried he wouldn't enjoy the quiet life after being so used to living it up in Helena all his life.

Richard waved a hand in the air. "They can visit, if that's what they want. They're all far too busy with business these days, except your sister who insists on living the high life, with no thought of marrying."

Olivia raised her eyebrows, but held back a chuckle. That sounded just like Cassandra. Living it up and doing whatever Cassandra wanted to do.

"Ooooooh." Olivia screamed. "I think the baby is coming," she said under her breath.

Joseph guided her back into the comfortable lounge chair and covered her with a blanket. "Just relax while I get Doc Spencer," he called over his shoulder and headed out the door.

"Pfffft, relax," she spat at his retreating back.

Richard had pots of water already boiling by the time Joseph arrived home with Doc Spencer. Olivia had already taken herself to bed, her legs wrapped around a pillow, trying to get comfortable. Richard had strolled to Mrs. Baker's cottage, with young Arthur strewn over his shoulder, knowing the older woman would want to be there for the birth.

"You know this is all your fault," Richard said to her when they returned to the house.

Mrs. Baker stared at him. "My fault? Blame your son-in-law, not me."

Joseph chuckled, listening to their banter as the two entered the front door. "You introduced them," Richard said, then waved Mrs. Baker into a chair.

"Did Richard tell you his news?" Joseph asked as he wandered around the room. Doc Spencer had banned him from the bedroom, and he felt at odds.

"News? What news?"

Richard lifted Arthur onto his lap. "I'm moving to Grand Falls. Now I have to decide where I'm going to live."

"You're always welcome here," Joseph said. Three years ago, he thought he'd never forgive Richard Seymour for the way he'd treated his daughter, and indeed, Joseph himself. But the man had repented, and it had made all the difference.

Richard shook his head. "Thank you for the offer, but that will never do. You and Olivia need your privacy, not the interference from a crotchety old man." He chuckled then, and Joseph knew he was right. "I will speak with Patrick and Harry. They will find somewhere quiet, but not too far away, for me to take roots."

Joseph knew he was right. He glanced about the room. Their home was more than he'd ever dreamed they would own, but Richard had become very upset when they tried to refuse his over-indulgent wedding gift.

A scream came from the bedroom, and Joseph stepped in that direction. "Sit down, Joseph. You know the doc won't let you in until after the baby comes." Mrs. Baker was right, but that didn't stop his anxiety.

The moment he sat, his son flew into his lap. "What's wrong with Mama?" he said, tears streaming down his little face.

"Mama is fine, but she will have a surprise soon." He held his son to his shoulder, and the small boy was asleep in minutes. All the excitement had taken it out of him.

Mrs. Baker suddenly stood. "I'll see if the doc needs any help," she said, and Joseph wished he could join her. Many screams and what seemed like forever later, she returned. "Your daughter has arrived," she told Joseph. "Doc says you can go in now." He handed Arthur off to his grandpapa and hurried to his wife.

Sitting on the edge of the bed, Joseph stroked Olivia's cheek. She held the baby in her arms. "What do you think about Esther for her name?" Joseph was overcome with emotion. Esther was his mother's name. "Esther Rose. My mother was Rose. I think it only fitting – Arthur after your father, Esther after my mother."

"It's perfect," he said, his voice full of emotion. "She's perfect too, just like her mother."

"Your wife needs to rest now," Doc Spencer said firmly. "Take the baby and let her rest." He handed Esther over and indicated for Joseph to leave.

He leaned in and kissed his wife's forehead. "I love you more than life itself," he whispered.

"I love you too," she said, then closed her eyes. A smile crossed her lips as she dozed off. Joseph could wait to show his new baby sister to young Arthur, and wondered how many more times he'd do the very same thing.

From the Author

Thank you for reading *Olivia*. I hope you enjoyed Olivia and Joseph's story as much as I enjoyed writing it. That brings the *Brides of Montana* series to an end.

Books in this series are as follows:

Emily

Grace

Victoria

Maggie

Callie

Olivia

To find out about new books, sign up for my newsletter at:

cheryl-wright.com/newsletter/

About the Author

Multi-published, award-winning and bestselling author Cheryl Wright, former secretary, debt collector, account manager, writing coach, and shopping tour hostess, loves reading.

She writes both historical and contemporary western romance, as well as romantic suspense.

She lives in Melbourne, Australia, and is married with two adult children and has six grandchildren. When she's not writing, she can be found in her craft room making greeting cards.

Links

Website: *http://www.cheryl-wright.com/*

Facebook Reader Group:
https://www.facebook.com/groups/cherylwrightauthor/

Join My Newsletter:

https://cheryl-wright.com/newsletter/

www.ingramcontent.com/pod-product-compliance
Lightning Source LLC
Chambersburg PA
CBHW070623120726
47909CB00004B/1304